MATTIE'S PLACE

Stories from a Country Diner

Written by
Howard Tuckey

Halo ●●●●
Publishing International
www.halopublishing.com

To contact the author Howard Tuckey
email: htuckey@stny.rr.com

Library of Congress Control Number: 201902277
ISBN 978-1-935268-73-4

Halo ●●●●
Publishing International
www.halopublishing.com

Printed in the United States of America

To my family, especially my wife, Dorie, who put up with this for so long without having me committed!

Stories from a Country Diner

Today's Specials

Stories from Mattie's Place

It ain't far from here to Mattie's Place, where you can get a great mug of coffee and a warm, homemade blueberry muffin, fresh-made any morning except Sunday. Mattie adds a hint of ginger, to make them special. They're good!

It's a place where you can sit back and enjoy yourself. The jukebox has been busted since the late 50's, but there's plenty of entertainment, as Doc Howland, Jim, Merle, and the rest of the regulars swap yarns and advice, and Mattie rides herd on all of them. Or you can just sit with your coffee and enjoy the good smells coming from the kitchen, where Dorie and Bump are helping Mattie fix today's specials. It seems like the whole town stops by at least once a day, so if you're looking for someone, chances are you'll find them here.

The chief denizen of Mattie's Place is a retired country sawbones, who just decided that none of the usual "retirement" spots appealed to him, so he stayed around these parts. It could be that Doc Howland is sweet on Mattie, or maybe it's the other way 'round. In any case, he's been a regular there since his wife passed on, and the booth he frequents, right at the end of the counter, has become known as "Doc's Corner." Judge Gordon even sends some of his odd cases over to talk to Doc to get 'em straightened out. Doc's a good listener, and has been known to arbitrate discussions, dispense advice (mostly from the Good Book), and even treat the minor bumps and bruises of life, although he's retired from his medical practice.

And sometimes Doc just sits and thinks, or writes, poetry mostly, but there *are* times it gets pretty lively in that corner booth, especially when Merle and the boys are holding forth.

Like one day last week …

Merle and the Old Indian Woman

"I think she's Sioux, or maybe Apache," Merle stopped for another gulp of Mattie's coffee, "some kind of Indian, anyway, but she's up to no good!"

Doc Howland leaned back, rubbed the side of his nose with the bit of his pipe, and shook his head. "This is New York, Merle, there's no Sioux or Apache here. Maybe Oneida or Mohawk?"

Merle wiped his chin. "Whatever, Doc. Anyway, I heard about this woman before. She walks into town from wherever she lives,"

"Over on Popple Hill," interjected Donnie. "I seen her over there last week."

Merle glared at him. "Hey, who's telling this? Even my *grand*kids know enough not to interrupt like that! Ain't you supposed to be loading hay bales or something?" He gulped the last of his coffee and gave Mattie the high sign for a refill. "Anyway, I heard how she'll hitch a ride, and then fall out of the vehicle just before you stop, so she can sue and collect damages from your insurance company."

"I heard that too," interjected Donnie, "they say that over to Sidney a few years back she collected a bundle from Walt Swager. He swore she fell out a'purpose, but it didn't do no good. Judge felt sorry for her."

Doc chuckled – "Old Judge Gordon never did feel sorry about too many folks. He's a real old-fashioned disciplinarian."

Donnie hesitated, digesting another of Doc's multi-syllable words. "Don't know about his religion," he said, "but he never felt sorry for *me*, no how! Had to sell my boat to pay the fine for making medicine up on the knob."

"You're lucky he didn't ship you off to Elmira," retorted Merle. "He went easy on you, that's for sure. Maybe he should have - might have learned you not to keep interrupting like that!"

"Well Merle," said Doc, "maybe you wouldn't get interrupted so much if you'd hurry up and get to the point."

"Aww, don't *you* start on me now, Doc," protested Merle, "you know I get tongue tied when you start pestering"

Then Mattie joined in the fray; "Are you jokers going to get any real work done today, or are you just going to set here and gab all morning? Say Donnie , aren't you supposed to be loading hay?"

"Merle's just about to set us straight on that old Indian woman," said Doc, holding out his mug for another refill. "Seems he's pretty well acquainted with her shenanigans."

"You mean Eva?" asked Mattie. "What's she up to now?"

Donnie broke in again; "I saw her the other morning! She was standing on the corner by the highway, waiting for the light to change so she could head on over the bridge, towards the dam."

"Yeah?" said Mattie.

"Well, she was carrying a fifty pound sack of dog feed from down to Greene's!"

"Then that wasn't Eva," said Mattie, "it was her daughter Carla. Eva might be walking, but she's not carrying much, ever since she fell out of Walt's car."

Donnie and Merle chimed in together, "Her daughter?

"Yes, her daughter's back from up by Syracuse, and she's living in that old abandoned trailer back of the clay banks" explained Mattie. "Now, do you want more coffee or no? I got other customers to tend to!"

Merle and Doc held out their mugs, but Donnie held his back and exclaimed, "But that's eight or nine miles! A fifty pound sack of dog feed!"

Mattie refilled Doc's and Merle's mugs, and waved the pot in Donnie's direction. "Yeah, fifty pounds. So? Hold your mug still! I've got to make a new pot, and I'm not going to dump this just so you can have fresh!"

"But fifty pounds! A woman! Up a hill!"

"Up *two* hills," corrected Doc, amused at Donnie's incredulity. "And two or three times a week!"

"But, but…"

"But, but my foot!" interjected Merle. "You're *still* butting in! You know, with a little practice you could get to be downright aggravating!"

Donnie sat back, mouth still open, trying to absorb all that about a woman carrying fifty pounds of dog feed up *two* hills, twice a week.

Merle just glared at him and said "Can I finish now, or do you want to discuss the weather while we're at it?" There was no response, so he plowed on. "I saw old Eva this morning, and I think she's into some new scam now."

"New scam?" said Doc, "How so?"

"Well," Merle mumbled, around a big bite of sugar donut, "I saw her over by Klute's Corners, just standing there with her walker, like she was waiting to cross." He gulped, swallowed, looked at Donnie as if daring him to butt in again, then continued. "I slowed down and waved her on across, but she just made a face at me and stood there, so I pulled on in to Penning's hardware store."

"So what's so mysterious about that?" broke in Mattie. "She maybe was headed to the Country Kitchen for breakfast."

"Well that's what *I* thought at first," said Merle, "but I looked back as I was getting out of my truck, and saw old man Geller coming down the road in his Caddy."

"Sounds about right," said Doc, "he usually heads down to the Big M to get his morning paper. Richest old skinflint in the county, and he won't have his paper delivered 'cause he doesn't want to tip the paperboy at Christmas time."

"Geez, Doc!" complained Merle, "now *you're* doing it!

"Just finish your story" said Mattie, "I've got to make that coffee!"

"Okay," Merle continued, "just as old man Geller turned the corner, she cranked that walker into high gear, and headed across right in front of him! That walker, stitching across the road like that, looked for all the world like my ex-wife's old Singer sewing machine!"

"Oh my," exclaimed Mattie, "did he hit her?"

"Nope," said Merle, "not this time. That Caddy almost rolled over, but he managed to miss her. Not that he would have hurt her much, at the speed he usually drives at."

"Gee, Doc," said Mattie, "you don't suppose…"

Doc could hardly contain his laughter; "Yes, I guess I do suppose. Rich old duffer in a Cadillac, driving slow, she tries to bounce off the side of it but her timing is off just a tad. Sounds like a real money maker to me!" He turned to Donnie. "You're quiet for a change – what's *your* take on it?"

"Fifty pounds? Nine miles up hill, twice a week?" Donnie mused – "Can she load a hay wagon?"

The End

Monday Afternoon at Sid's

Doc was laughing as he walked in the front door of Mattie's. "Some folks were just born to complain, I guess," he said to no one in particular. He headed toward his customary corner booth. Marie – the new waitress – followed him with his mug and a pot of hi-test.

"Who's complaining now?" she asked, as she poured him a cup.

"Well," Doc said, as most of the heads in the diner turned to hear what was so funny, "I was over at Sid's for an oil change when I heard old Myron Kresge, fit to be tied as usual, hollering at Wally." He blew on his coffee to cool it off, and took a sip. "Wally was holding his own, but I don't know how long he'd have been able to keep his cool if Sid hadn't stepped in…"

"But Mr. Kresge, it's been over a month since we changed that tire for you, and I know the left rear hubcap was missing then. I even asked you about it…"

"Don't try to make excuses, boy, I know shoddy work when I see it! I want my hubcap back where it belongs!" The old man stood glowering at Wally, waving his cane at the rear of the tan 1948 DeSoto, and pointing at the offending cap-less wheel. "I want that cap replaced now! And no argument about it, or I'll call my attorney!"

"What seems to be the problem here, Mr. Kresge?" Sid came out of the store- room, wiping his hands on a grease rag. “Wally may be young, but he’s proven himself to be very dependable. He’s one of my best employees, in fact, and if he says the cap was already missing when he changed the tire, well, I’m inclined to take his word for it.”

“You may call him dependable, but I say he’s negligent!” wheezed the red-faced old man. “He’s lost my hub cap and I want it back! Car looks terrible without it!”

Sid looked over the old DeSoto, noting all the rust and dings, including the one Mr. Kresge had once tried to blame on him. The blue paint in the dent still matched the blue paint on Mr. Kresge’s garage door frame. “You’re right, it does look terrible, but I think we might be able to help you out, just this once.” He hollered toward the storeroom door, just on the other side of the bay where the DeSoto was sitting. “Hey Charlie! Remember that cap you found over by the tracks the other day? I think it might be the one for this car. Is it still on the shelf in there?”

Charlie popped up out of nowhere, it seemed, right beside the old man’s car. “Yep, here ‘tis, and I’ll be doggoned if it don’t look like the right cap!”

Sid examined the cap and nodded, “Sure does, don’t it!” He bent down by the wheel and popped it into place, then stood back and said “Look at that -- it’s a perfect match with the one on the front. Guess this is our lucky day!”

Mr. Kresge blinked and scowled, and looked perplexed, almost disappointed, now that today’s irritation had been smoothed over so easily. “Well, I guess, but you’d better watch these kids a little closer! Poor way to do business! Never make it in this world running your business that way! Got to be able to depend on your help.” He got in the car, still shaking his head and muttering. He started it, ground it into gear, and backed out of the bay, just barely missing Mrs. Jones’ Caddy in the process.

Wally looked from Sid to Charlie and back again. "I'm confused. When did Charlie find a hubcap? And how did it turn out to be the right one for that old DeSoto?"

Charlie grinned, and Sid chuckled "He didn't!" He chuckled again at Wally's expression. "That was the cap Charlie just now popped off the *right* rear! I'm hoping the old coot will stop in for service over at the Sunoco before he notices that one's missing."

Doc leaned back in the booth, and held out his mug out for a warm-up. "Like I said, some folks were just born to complain!"

The End

Chinese Buffet

Doc stopped in for breakfast this morning, and Mattie met him at the door, with a letter in her hand. "Boy am I glad to see you! Merle and Donny have been driving me crazy already this morning. They want me to open this and read it to them. But I told them it's addressed to you, and it was none of their business." She handed him the letter and said "Go ahead on over, and I'll bring th ... Merle! Don't you dare drop that pot! Are you in so much of a hurry that you can't wait for him to set down!?

Merle grinned sheepishly, and said "Just trying to help. You looked like you might could use a break, so I brung it over. Donny had to go over to Sid's for a minute, but he'll be right back. Is it from Jim? What'd he say? How's he doing? Did he get his stitches out yet?"

Doc started laughing. "I see what you mean, Mattie. But maybe I'll just take this on home and read it there in peace and quiet." He winked at Mattie, and chuckled when Merle almost choked on his coffee. "Naw, guess I'll just read it here. My, looks like he wrote several pages here. Hope everything's okay."

"Me too," agreed Mattie, "looks like more than usual. Guess that's what got these two lunkheads stirred up, and I must admit, I'm kind of curious too."

"Okay," said Doc, as he slit the envelope with his pocket knife. "Here comes Donny back, and I can't hold off all three of you, so let me get started on a sticky bun and a cup of coffee, and we'll check it out."

The four of them settled into Doc's favorite corner booth, and he started reading. "MmmmHmmm. Ahh. Well yes, I would too!"

They all jumped when a voice cried out. "Out loud! Read it out loud, you cantankerous old booger!" Doc looked over the back of the booth, and there was old Henry Talcott, straining for all he was worth to hear what Jim's letter had to say.

"Come on over here and join us, Henry," laughed Doc, "no sense in putting your neck out of joint trying to hear this. Move in and make some room, Donny." He read down through the first few lines, and said "Nothing really new here, tests all came back okay, and now he's going to take a couple of days to go on down toward the city to see his cousins while he's down that way."

"That's all? He used up three, four pages just to say that?"

"No, Henry, there's more. Lessee – might as well just read it like he wrote it. That make you happy?" They all nodded, and Doc started reading what big Jim had written:

"Hey Doc, remember that Chinese buffet I told you about the last time I came down here? I stopped there for lunch today, after I got my test results. Thought I might celebrate a little. Well, this particular restaurant is just about half-way between health department closings, so I knew it would be a pretty good balance between ptomaine and good eats. The department had closed it several months ago, only because the inspector had been driving by on the highway behind the restaurant and spotted a couple hundred frozen chickens thawing out (unwrapped) on the roof, right out in the open. Definite no-no there. But now it's open again, 'under new management', and still one of my favorite places to eat lunch.

Anyway, I had just sat down to my usual first course – a Mongolian hot plate, a bowl of hot and sour soup, and a dish of kim-chee, when a tour bus full of elderly Chinese folks from New York City pulled into the parking lot, and about 75 of them poured into the place.

It's a big restaurant, so there was just about enough room for all of them, except for one wrinkled, shabbily dressed old man who looked lost, and it was obvious that the rest of the bus folks were okay with that state of affairs. Every time he'd head towards a likely looking spot at a table, it would close up, and they would not-look at him. It wasn't just that they didn't notice him, or see him. It was more of an obvious choice to not-look, if you know what I mean.

He just stood there looking helpless, and I felt bad taking up a whole booth by myself while he just stood there, so I motioned for him to join me. He looked around, not certain that I was looking at him, so I nodded and pointed to the seat across from me. He lit up like the sun coming out on a cloudy day, and came and sat down, nodding and smiling all the way, and began to thank me. At least I gathered that's what he was doing – I recognized right off that we had a language barrier here. He apparently had no English at all, and my Mandarin is even more of a no-show, but we had smiles in common, so I figured we'd get along pretty good.

Then a woman (one of the group's leaders, I think) came stomping over, looking Very Official, and said something not so nice (also not sure because of the language, but the tone was unmistakable), and the sun went out. She turned and began to apologize in almost understandable English to me, for his unseemly behavior, and he slowly started to slide out of the booth. I reached out and put my hand on his arm and stopped him, motioned for him to sit down again, and politely told her I had, in fact, invited him to sit there, and she should please learn to mind her own business and show a little more respect for us older folks.

He smiled and lit up again, and she just stood there with her mouth opening and closing, looking for all the world like the koi in the tank behind her. Then she turned and went away, and I noticed the folks at the nearby tables and booths started not-looking at both of us.

By this time the crowd at the buffet had thinned out, so I motioned for him to go and get something to eat. He looked confused at that, so I took him by the arm and led him over to the food, and helped him get some fried rice and soup.

We sat together in silence, enjoying our meal, not conversing (except with an occasional smile) and then he reached in his jacket pocket and took out a picture. When he showed it to me I could tell it was his family because of the way his eyes shone as he pointed to them. He said these were his grandkids, and he was on his way to see them. Don't ask me how I knew for sure what he was saying, because he said it in his language. I only recognized the pride and the love, not the words themselves. I've got grandkids myself, after all. When he pointed to the pretty young woman standing with him in the one picture his voice broke a little, and I guessed that it was his wife, and that she had passed on.

Then he made me understand he wanted to see *my* family as well, and I took out pictures of my wife and kids and grandkids, and showed him, and he lit right up again and he told me they were beautiful too. Then when I pointed at Ellen and shook my head, he realized that we had much more in common than we had first thought. He put his hand on my arm and closed his eyes for a few seconds, squeezing out a tear in the process.

We went back to eating in silence mostly, with a few smiles when we compared things on our plates, nodding in agreement over how good things were, and went back for plenty of seconds. He was hungry, and ate almost as much as I did! I finished my lunch and got ready to leave, and got up and reached over to shake hands with him. He struggled to his feet and said the first and only English words I heard him say – "Thank you!" Well, that turned the handshake into a bear-hug, and all the not-looking people started to not-stare instead!

I went out through the foyer, paid for our lunches on the way, and went out to my truck, parked just outside the window. I got in and fastened my seatbelt, started the truck, and looked up to see him standing in the window, smiling and waving goodbye, just like a little kid. Then I turned to back out, had to blink more than a few times before I could see clearly, and drove away."

Doc refolded the letter, and started putting it back in the envelope. "Sounds like him, doesn't it? Always picking up strays and such, and ... wait, what's this? Ha! This must be from his fortune cookie. Lessee ..." He chuckled and nodded, "Yep, they sure gave him the right cookie this time."

He handed it to Mattie, and she read it to them: "Get ready to greet a new friend today."

The End

BOOMSPLAT!

It was the third day of the county fair, and as usual it was the topic of conversation at Mattie's Place. Doc looked over at the end of the counter and saw Fernal, just sitting there by himself, grinning as if he had heard something really funny.

"Hey, Fernal! Gonna let us in on that joke? Looks like it was a pretty good one," says Doc.

Fernal turned around, still laughing, and allowed as how he went to the fair the night before, and naturally had to tour along the row of old tractors. The big old orange Oliver caught his eye, and he got to thinking about his grandpa and the old Oliver tractor he used to have.

"He used to park it under the shed roof that hung off the back of the barn. That old tractor was sometimes a little hard to start, but he had a battery starter on it, and he kept the charger plugged in. If he had the throttle and choke set just right it would start up with a bang.

"There was just one thing about that bang, though. He had a vertical exhaust stack on that tractor, and no real muffler to speak of. Those who know about such things might remember that if you didn't cover the pipe when you shut the tractor off, it would suck cold air down the pipe and warp the exhaust valves. That wasn't good for the tractor at all.

"So he would put a tin can over top of the pipe to cut off the air."

Donny broke in, and said "I remember we had an old Ford that got the valves warped when we started it without the manifold pipe, and ..."

"Donny," said Doc, "I'm going to put a can over *your* head if you don't stop interrupting!" Donny looked sheepish (as only Donny can, 'cause he's had a lot of practice), and Fernal nodded to Doc and picked up where he'd left off.

"Well, if whoever started the tractor forgot to take the can off the pipe, the bang would launch it clear to the roof! In this case, that was all of three feet, which didn't leave much reaction time to duck. The can would bounce back off the underside of the roof and then ricochet off the noggin of whoever was nearest. I could show you scars!

"After observing that cannon shot effect a couple of times, it's no surprise that me and my cousin surmised that we might just be able to use it to launch other things. We pretended it was a mortar, on account of the Korean War was going on, and we were kind of fascinated by those things then.

"So it's also no surprise that we kind of experimented with the first thing at hand. In this case the first thing at hand just happened to be a rotten potato that had rolled out of the corner of the hog pen. It was just far enough out of reach that it was just lying there in all its stinking glory. There's not another smell on earth quite as nasty and long lasting as a rotten potato. And it just fit (with a little bit of pressure) down that old Oliver exhaust stack.

"Only problem was that the Oliver had set there for a couple of days, and it was sometimes a little cranky about starting after it had set, and it just wouldn't fire. We didn't want to run the battery down, 'cause grandpa wouldn't appreciate that at all. Not even a little.

"So we tried to fish the potato out of the stack, but all we managed to do was slice it up a little (it was pretty runny anyway) and it got lodged even further down the pipe. So we replaced the can, and forgot about it.

"Well, that evening grandpa wanted to rake some hay he'd cut a few days before, and he wanted us to help load it on the hay wagon. We didn't use a baler then, just piled it in the hay-mow after it got real dry.

"He took the can off the stack and tried to start the tractor. Wouldn't start. Cranky. So he primed the carburetor, which meant pouring a little gas into the top of it, and then hitting the starter button. This was a little tricky, and sometimes you got a little more than a "bang" -- more like a 'BOOM!'
"He got a little more than a 'BOOM' – actually it was more like 'BOOMSPLAT!', or to be even more accurate, 'BOOMSPLAT-SPLATTER!' That was followed by a few seconds of silence, then the awfullest gagging and cussing I ever heard in my short life. Which I was certain wasn't going to get any longer if he ever caught up to us!"

Fernal took another swig of coffee, held out his mug for a refill, and grinned again. "I stood there looking at that old Oliver just like grandpa's, at the fairgrounds last evening, and all I could think of was "BOOM-SPLAT!"

The End

How Bump Got His Nickname

Mattie was wiping down the counter, singing "Rain, rain, go away, come again some other day," when the front door slammed open.

Mike Doohan ducked in, shaking off the rain, and apologized for letting the door go like that.

Pete, the old breakfast cook, stuck his head out of the kitchen to see what the ruckus was all about, and looked out the front door. "Look at it come down," he exclaimed, "like..."

"...a cow peeing on a flat rock!" the regulars chimed in and finished for him.

Pete looked disgusted. "Guess I'll have to think up a new one."

"You didn't think up *that* one, Bump!" shouted someone from the end of the counter. "You heard it on the TV!" There was a ripple of laughter in agreement.

The old cook was brewing up a retort when the door slammed open again, propelled by a gust of wind, and admitted a bedraggled individual who looked like he had crawled all night to get there. "Gawl-dang it Bump!" hollered Maynard, as he pushed the door shut. "Even Superman couldn't fly across that parking lot without getting his S wet!" He grinned at the old cook, wet his finger, and made a score mark in the air.

"I give up!" said Pete, and retreated back into the kitchen.

"Hey Pete," hollered Vern, "when you gonna tell us how's come they call you 'Bump'?"

The swinging door to the kitchen cut off the cook's muttered reply, and the usual round of laughter followed. It was always fun for some of the guys to pick on Pete.

"I'd be careful who I got riled up, if I were you." Mattie looked directly at Vern. "Don't you know it's never a good idea to get on the cook's bad side?"

"Aw, we're just having fun," protested Vern, "don't mean nothing by it." He held out his mug for a refill. "Besides, his own cousin is the one that told us his nickname in the first place."

"Yeah," chimed in Maynard, "but he never told us how he came by it."

"Don't matter," said Mattie. "I think it's funny too, but Pete gets embarrassed, and then he gets grumpy, and I'd like to see *you* try to work with him after you guys get him going. And if you think I'm kidding, just ask Donnie how come he was walking funny last week." They all turned to look at Donnie, who busied himself in the newspaper, trying to ignore them.

The swinging door opened again, and Doc Howland came through, his wet shoes squishing as he walked. "I had to park out back, so I came through the kitchen so as not to drown. It's raining out there, if you hadn't noticed." He headed for his private booth, nodding at the crowd. "What's up with Pete? He just growled when I said hello." He looked straight at Donnie and Maynard. "You boys been ragging on him again?" Mattie followed him with a mug and a fresh pot of coffee. "What else?" She frowned towards the miscreants. "They keep picking on him about his nickname. One of these days he'll get even, though, and the laugh'll be on the other foot."

Doc just looked at her and smiled at the malaphor. "Yes, old Pete *has* been known to get even, yes he has."

"How's that?" Vern looked alarmed. "Whaddya mean, 'get even?"

"Ohh, nothing serious," said Doc, looking over at Donnie. "Just a little extra in your chocolate chip cookies, or a special piece of chocolate meringue pie, maybe. Nothing serious," he repeated, and smiled again.

Donnie looked uncomfortable. "I didn't mean nothin' by it," he said, "just carryin' on with the other guys..."

"And never once considering the possibility that it might be upsetting to old Pete," admonished Doc. "I ain't sticking up for the old codger's method of revenge, but I think a lesson was learned there."

"I guess it was," allowed Donnie, "but I'd still like to know how he come to be called 'Bump'."

"Yeah," echoed the rest of the guys. "When did they start calling him that?"

"Mattie?" Doc looked at her inquisitively.

"Nope," she replied. "*You* tell 'em yourself. And I'm not responsible for what happens, either!"

"Okay," said Doc, turning to face the group of questioning faces. "But not a word of this leaves this diner. Understood?"

All eagerly nodded yes, and Doc re-armed himself with a fresh mug of coffee and started:

"About thirty years ago, when Pete's wife was still alive, and their daughter Sally was eight or nine, they decided to remodel their house. They put in new cabinets in the kitchen, and a real shower in the bathroom. Evvie wanted genuine wall-to-wall carpeting in the living room, but Pete disagreed, and fought tooth and nail against the idea. He eventually came around to their way of thinking, though, and they went out and bought some real pretty carpeting from the discount store. He even rented one of those knee kicker things to stretch the carpet with.

"Well, they moved out all the furniture, and put a long wire on the TV antenna so they wouldn't miss Lawrence

Welk, and Pete proceeded to tear up the old linoleum and pull all the nails that stuck up from the floor. Then he started unrolling the carpet, cutting and fitting it as he went. He really got into it, and was real proud of the way it was going. It was hell on the knees, though, and he just knew he'd be limping for life after he got it all done. It actually took him near six weeks for all the bruises on his knees to clear up.'

Donnie said, "Been there, done that." He looked over at Vern and nodded, "Remember the time we had with the rugs over at the funeral parlor?"

Doc glared him into silence. "Can't resist butting in no how, can you?" He continued, trying to ignore the interruption. "Anyway, Pete worked right through lunch time – only grabbed a quick sandwich -- and never even stopped for a smoke. That's how determined he was to get it all done that afternoon. One more short wall and he was finished, and he sat down and leaned against the door casing to survey his handiwork.

"He must've figured it was time for a smoke, and reached for the pack in his shirt pocket, but it wasn't there. Just about that time his eye caught on a bump in the carpet, near dead center in the room. He got up and walked over to it, all the time knowing that he wasn't going to tear up all that work for a lousy pack of Lucky Strikes. He just stared at the bump for a minute, cussed a blue streak, and proceeded to stomp it flat. I mean, he really took out all his frustration on that one little bump, and when he was finished with that spot it looked just like the rest of the room. Nice and flat.

"About that time, Evvie came running in to see what all the ruckus was about. He had quieted down by this time, so she just told him the carpet looked real nice, and she really liked it.

"She handed him his Luckies, and said he'd left them on the kitchen counter.

"Then she asked him if he'd seen Sally's hamster."

The End

Lonnie

Mattie's Place was quiet, even for a Monday morning. The few regulars studied their coffee, or ate in silence. Even Dave, who normally whistled and sang as he ran the dishwasher, seemed subdued. Mattie picked up the pot and quietly offered refills, but only Doc Howland held out his mug, nodding his thanks. "Quite a change from Thursday," he said, looking around at the nearly empty diner, "S'pose everyone got enough to eat?"

Mattie flashed a brief, tired smile, and nodded back at him. "I think so," she said, "hope so, anyway." She brightened a little as she remembered the crowd that had filled the place for her annual free Thanksgiving dinner. "Merle and Cliff seemed to be enjoying their waiter jobs, and I thought I was gonna cry when the Turner kids brought me that homemade thank you card."

"You *did* cry, you old softie," accused Doc. "I saw you with shiny eyes more than once."

"Well you did your share too," she smiled. "I got a picture this year of you carving up the turkey, and Cliff serving it to old Emma, and the Durden family saying grace and mentioning our names. And all the delivery boxes we packed for Jim and Lon…" She stopped short, and turned away to hide her grief. But her shoulders hunched as she sobbed, and she leaned heavily into the counter. "Why Lonnie?" She turned back as Doc rose quickly to comfort her. "Why him? Why Thanksgiving, of all days?"

"Well," said Doc, steering her gently into the booth, where he sat across from her, "it was just his time, I guess. Everyone knew his heart wasn't all that strong. And remember we thought he was a goner a couple of years ago. I think even *he* knew he was living on borrowed time."

"But he was so sweet and simple," she sobbed, "never more than a child's mind in him. He'd always come and offer to run errands, or help Dud clean up in the evening. And I don't know of anyone who ever had a bad word for him."

"I know," said Doc, "Lonnie was always wanting to help someone. And you know on Thanksgiving he was doing exactly what made him happiest – helping make people smile."

Mattie looked up at Doc. "I know, but the *Dorgans*? After the way their kids treated him, and the old man too? They're nothing but…"

"People," finished Doc. "All Lonnie knew is they're people. And as far as he was concerned, people are to be loved, no matter what. Remember what he used to say about 'created in God's image'."

"But those kids are incorrigible!" Mattie was angry now, as she thought more about it. "They threw ice balls at him a couple of weeks ago, remember? He needed stitches over his eye! Old Man Dorgan laughed and said he shoulda ducked! And Lonnie just let it go."

"I know, I know," said Doc, "they were the *last* people you or I would have thought kindly of at Thanksgiving, or *any* day. Let 'em starve in that old rundown shanty. Or freeze. But Lonnie saw 'em as people, and good or bad, people, to him, shouldn't go hungry. He thought no differently of them than he did anyone else. So he took them some Thanksgiving dinner."

"And his heart quit on the long walk back."

"Yes, his heart quit," said Doc, "but his love didn't."

Mattie looked at him quizzically, "What do you mean his love didn't?"

Doc poured them both fresh coffee, and answered. "Well, on Saturday as I was leaving the funeral parlor I saw old man Dorgan and his wife coming in. They were acting real quiet and shy, like they didn't want to be noticed. He said that they'd come to pay their respects."

"Come to pay their respects?" Mattie snorted in disbelief. "They never had any respect for anyone before in their life! Never bothered with any funerals, nor even church, for that matter."

"Well, Mattie," said Doc, "that's just it, now. I ran into Pastor Wells yesterday afternoon, and he told me that the whole Dorgan family showed up at church bright and early yesterday morning all dressed up in their best clean clothes, and asked if they could please come in. Well, Pastor Wells was as surprised as could be, but he said they sure could, and he started the service with some mighty unfamiliar folks setting right there in the second pew, just as big as life.

"He was even more surprised when he asked for folks to stand up and tell how they'd been blessed lately, on account of it was Thanksgiving and all, and old man Dorgan and his wife slowly stood to their feet. He tried to talk, but his voice was cracking pretty badly. It took him a minute to get to where he could talk so they could hear him, and Pastor said it was apparent that he was struggling with what he wanted to say. But everybody was so quiet you could hear his heart beating, almost. He was almost whispering when he said that they wanted to come to church there because they knew that it was Lonnie's church, and so it must be special.

"Mister Dorgan said that Lonnie's taking a meal out to them, especially after how they'd treated him, had really had an effect on them. Seems he and his wife had gone to church when they were younger, but something happened that gave them the idea that everybody was hypocrites and so they stopped going. They'd think about going every once in a while, but would think about them hypocrites, and they'd start acting all mean and cantankerous again. He said they figured nobody ever cared for them or their family, so why should they care about church? Or anyone else, for that matter?"

Mattie had tears in her eyes again. "Then along comes Lonnie," she whispered.

"Then along comes Lonnie," nodded Doc, "and his simple, honest act of charity really touched them all. The old man was crying by this time, and so was most everyone else in the service, including Pastor Wells. Mr. Dorgan said that he and his whole family were sorry for the way they'd treated people, especially Lonnie – and he broke down and wept for a little bit, until Pastor Wells, and a couple of other folks who'd had run-ins with the Dorgans came up and put their arms around them. Even the kids were crying by then, and the youngest Dorgan girl just hung on to Mrs. Wells and sobbed. I guess it was quite a time.

"Pastor Wells said he'd had a real nice message to give them yesterday morning, but he told them what they'd just seen and heard was better than any sermon *he* could have given them. In fact, he said he realized now that Lonnie had been *living* better sermons in front of *all* of us for quite some time, in the little things he used to do. And it was finally beginning to take effect."

Mattie wiped her eyes and got up to wait on a new customer. She stopped at the end of the counter and looked back. "You know, Doc," she smiled, "I think maybe *I'd* better start remembering some of Lonnie's sermons too. Do you suppose they've got a pew for *me*?"

"I think probably they do," nodded Doc, smiling; "I'll save you a place right next to me!"

The End

Charlie Learns A Lesson

The string of Christmas bells on the front door jangled as the old man came in and stomped the snow off his boots. He headed for the coat hooks at the end of the first booth to hang up his hat and threadbare jacket. A chorus of "Morning Charlie" followed him to his seat at the counter, and Mattie arrived with a mug of hot coffee just as he sat down.

"Hi, Charlie," she said, "oatmeal will be ready in a minute. You want a banana on it this morning?" She gave him an unanswered smile, and rearranged the newspaper on the counter.

"Yeah, I guess," he replied, "maybe a glass of OJ too. I feel a cold coming on." Mattie nodded and headed for the kitchen. Charlie glanced at the paper beside him, made a face, and muttered something to himself.

"Say what, Charlie? came a voice from the booth next to him.

"Hi, Doc," he turned and nodded, "just mumbling to myself." He gestured toward the Town Reporter lying on the counter. "Paper's full of folks trying to play on sympathy, now it's Christmas again. Never had much use for all that folderol – let 'em work like everyone else. Always asking for a handout." He kind of folded in on himself again, and contemplated his coffee.

Doc got up and helped himself to a refill, and freshened up Charlie's mug as well. The old man thanked him, and as he sat back down, Doc said "Well, I guess some of 'em really need a hand, 'specially this time of year, with the fuel prices and all. And the price of kids' clothes for even a small family – not too many jobs left around here that pay enough to be stylish at all. And after the bare necessities, ain't nothing left for candy 'n toys, 'n all the fun stuff that the kids like so much."

"Candy and toys?" Charlie set his mug down and looked at Doc. "We never got candy and toys when I was a kid. Always had to work. Christmas, Thursday, Saturday, one day's same as another as far as we knew."

The bells on the door interrupted him about then, and everyone turned to see who had joined the crowd. It was the new youth pastor from the Community Church, with one of his kids.

"Hi Pastor Fred," called out someone from the other end of the counter, "and hi Freddie!" The pastor's six-year-old son turned and smiled shyly at them, and someone made the inevitable joke about "those two front teeth showing up in your stocking on Christmas morning." Mattie reached in the jar and dug out two lollipops, "One's for Katie," she admonished.

"Hi, Mattie,,, guys," said the pastor. "Just out picking up the donations for the needy families at the center."

Charlie turned back to Doc, and shook his head. "See what I mean? Donations! *We* had to work to eat. Kids today don't know about going without like we did. I never asked for no handout, always had to work for what I got. And I never had nobody give me a lollipop, neither. Did get one once, but me and my sister had to take turns licking it 'til it was gone,,," his voice trailed off as he realized others were staring at him. Charlie was a little hard of hearing, and his voice tended to get a little louder when he was complaining, and this was no exception. Doc had tried to shush him down so everyone else in the place wouldn't hear, especially the pastor, but to no avail.

There was an embarrassed silence for a few seconds, as folks tried to sort out what they'd just heard. Mattie reached under the counter and brought out the box of food and stuff that they'd collected in the diner. Pastor Fred just smiled and thanked her for it, then turned to go. "C'mon Freddie," he said, "we've got a few more stops to make. Merry Christmas, everybody, and thank you all!"

Someone opened the door for him and he started out, then stopped and turned when Freddie said "Wait daddy, I need to do something."

The little guy turned and went back into the diner, and shyly approached the counter where Charlie was sitting, head down, intently studying his coffee. Freddie held out his hand and said "Mister? Sir? Here, you can have *my* lollipop. I've still got one for Sissy, and she prob'ly won't eat it all anyway, and I can finish hers, but this one is for you." He laid the candy on the counter when Charlie didn't respond, and said "Merry Christmas, sir." Then he turned and ran outside and rejoined his dad.

The diner was dead quiet now, with everyone either staring at Charlie, or busy blowing an assorted collection of noses into an even more assorted collection of handkerchiefs and bandanas. Charlie sat there, still as a stump, for just a few more seconds, then got up and walked out the door.

"Hey Charlie -- you forgot your coa,,," called Mattie, and Doc held up his hand, then pointed out the window to where Pastor Fred was just closing the trunk of his battered Ford. There was the old man kneeling in the snow beside it, with his arms wrapped around a little boy, his head bowed onto the boy's shoulder. Pastor Fred was standing there nodding and smiling as he watched what his son had accomplished with his simple, innocent gesture.

"Better refill that mug, Mattie," said Doc. "He's going to need some more coffee when he comes back in. And you know, it looks like little Freddie has got himself another grampa in the bargain!"

The End

Grammatical Ambiguity

"Clifford! What in thunderation did you do, go off your diet?" Harlow turned from the bulletin board in Mattie's Place and hollered down the counter. He grinned and winked at Mattie, as if to say, "watch this one," then ignored the exasperated look she gave him. He turned back to the board. "You must have," he continued, "according to this!"

Poor Clifford looked as if he wanted to crawl under the counter and hide. Harlow was always poking fun at him, and as good-natured as Clifford was, it still made him blush beet red.

Harlow adjusted his bifocals just for effect, and looked at the board. "*Farmall tractor for sale*," he read aloud, running his finger over the words. He looked down at Clifford, then back along the counter, making sure he had everyone's attention, making the most of yet another opportunity to have some fun at the redhead's expense. He put on his most studious expression, and turned back to the notice. "*Farmall tractor for sale by private owner with extra weight in the rear.*" He started laughing, and a few of the guys joined in, some of them not quite sure just why. "Extra weight in the rear! Whatcha think about that one, Doc?"

Doc Howland smiled, and shook his head, then waved Clifford over to his private booth, rescuing him from further embarrassment. "C'mon over here, Cliff, and I'll buy you another coffee."

Cliff slunk over, grateful to be invited into the corner booth, out of direct attention of the rest. "What's he talking about, Doc?" The poor guy was genuinely confused. "It's just I needed some extra cash for a Christmas present for Wilma, and I got another tractor, so I figured I'd let that one go, and throw in the wheel weights…"

"Oh, it's not just the Farmall, or the wheel weights," said Doc, "it's just the way the notice was *worded* that could be a bit confusing. The way you put it, it sounded like the *owner* was the one with the extra weight. You've got to put your words and punctuation in the right places, or it can change the meaning something awful!"

"Punctuation? You mean commas and suchlike? I was never no good at them."

"Yep," nodded Doc, "commas and suchlike. They've got to be in the right places, or it can get real ambiguous in a hurry."

"Oh." Clifford studied his coffee for a bit, then looked up Doc, who was busy refilling his old briar pipe. "Um, Doc?"

Doc looked up, a twinkle in his eye, already anticipating the next question. "Yes, Clifford?"

"Umm, what's am… ambiggeus?"

"Am*big*uous," corrected Doc. And he nodded, as if satisfied with that pronunciation. "Well, it's when you say something, or write something and mean one thing, but it comes out sounding like something else. It can make for some interesting goings on. In fact, sometimes grammatical ambiguity can be downright aggravating!" He thought that one over again, and repeated, "Yes sir, grammatical ambiguity. That's as good a way to put it as any, I guess."

"C'mon, Doc," pleaded Clifford, "you're messing up my head with all them big words. You're just having fun with me again. What's it mean?"

"Nope, not picking a bit." Doc smiled, and thought for a minute, and said, "OK, Cliff, it's this way. Take poor old Barlow Farnsworth, up in Cortland County for example..."

About this time Donnie, who had been listening in all this time, broke in. "I know old man Farnsworth! Used to haul silage for him, back wh..." His voice trailed off as he realized he'd interrupted again, and Doc was glaring at him.

"Anyway," resumed Doc, with an exasperated look on his face, "Barlow and one of his slower sons was mending fence, and he says 'Cletus, I'm gonna line up this corner post, and when I nod my head, you hit it.' "

Cliff thought about that, and his eyes widened at the implications of it.

"You guessed it, Clifford," said Doc, "Barlow's lucky Cletus is not only dim-witted, but nearsighted too. And Cletus is lucky his old man couldn't run all that fast with a busted shoulder. And Old Hercules (that was Barlow's Angus bull) was lucky the fence didn't get fixed. And that afternoon several of the heifers over in the next pasture proceeded to get lucky as well."

Clifford's eyes kept getting wider hearing Doc recite that chain of events. "So what happened, Doc?"

"So I guess everybody got out of it okay, except for the following Sunday, when Barlow was driving to church with his arm out the window on account of the cast. Old Deacon Yates was just turning the corner and saw him, and thought he was signaling to turn *left,* up towards the *Methodist* church,,,"

Donnie broke in again, "But Barlow don't go to the Meth... sorry"

Doc never looked at Donnie – just rolled his eyes and continued – "As I was about to say, Barlow's on the board of deacons up at Disciples of Christ, along with Deacon Yates." He glared at Donnie again. "And old Deacon Yates thought he had backslid or something and just stared at him in disbelief, and never saw old Hercules (he'd got out again) standing dead center in the road.

"They had a roast beef dinner right after the funeral."

The End

Jasper Gets Even

Mattie turned from the window and grabbed the coffee pot. "Anybody want a refill?" She started down the counter sloshing hot java into the row of lifted mugs, never spilling a drop.

"Over here, too, Mattie," came a call from the corner booth, accompanied by a waving mug.

"Keep your shirt on, Merle – I know *you* do, but it looks as if you'll have to wait for the next pot – unless you want decaf." She looked at the one denizen of the booth not waving his mug; "Doc? Decaf or regular today?"

"I'll wait for regular, Mattie, I think I could use the real thing this morning, thanks."

"You do look kind of tuckered, Doc," said Merle, "how come? Up late last night?"

"You might say that," nodded Doc, "yes, you might say that." He acted as if he was ready to elaborate, when the bell on the front door rang, and Mike Doohan slouched in.

"Hey Doo! Got the day off?" hollered someone from the end of the counter. "Where's LeeRoy?"

"'Lo," returned the big Irishman, "LeeRoy ain't feeling too good right now. Sent me in for coffee and donuts." He looked around the diner, as if he was looking for someone in particular, and looked a little disappointed that he didn't see him. "Anybody seen Jasper this morning?"

There was a chorus of "Not yet," and "Nope" from around the room. Doc just stuck his nose into his nearly empty mug and said nothing.

Doo picked up the order Mattie brought out of the kitchen, and stopped at the register. "Well if you do, tell him LeeRoy wants to see him." Pulling his cap back down over his eyes he left without another word.

It wasn't long before a sorry-looking individual came in through the back door, looking like death warmed over. He looked around for a few seconds, and croaked "Hey Doc! you busy?"

"Jasper! Where you been?" hollered a couple of the boys. "And what's that smell? Ain't it a little early for trapping skunks?"

Jasper waved off their questions and made his way back to the corner booth, where Doc and Merle went out of their way to make room for him. "I done it, Doc!" he whispered.

"I gathered as much," returned the doc, trying to talk while holding his breath. "Now why don't you get on home and try that tomato juice like I told you?"

"Just wanted to make sure it was tomato juice and baking soda," said Jasper. "Is that right?"

"Yes," gasped Doc, "now get on out of here before you suffocate us all! And try soaking in the pond for a while – maybe that'll help too!"

Jasper left by the back door, just as Mattie got back to the booth with fresh coffee and one of those "Now-what-in-blazes-is-going-on?" looks on her face.

Doc finally got his breath back and started to laugh, knowing he was on the hook for an explanation. "Okay, take a break and I'll let you in on the secret," he said, "but you have to promise you won't say anything to LeeRoy!"

"Not a word," whispered Mattie, and Merle nodded in agreement.

"Okay. Remember earlier this spring when Jasper's daughter Janie moved back in with him?" Both heads nodded again, and Doc continued. "Well, she had some furniture to store, and LeeRoy had just finished building his new storage units up by the garage."

"Yeah," said Merle, "I helped float the concrete for the floors."

"Well," continued Doc, ignoring the interruption, "Janie rented one of LeeRoy's new storage units and loaded it full of nice new furniture. Was going to move it into their new house when it's finished.'

"Was?" asked Mattie, isn't she still going to move it in?"

"Well," said Doc, "when she went to get some of it out, she found that it had all been spoiled by some kind of mold and mildew, and they think it was from the new concrete not being fully cured when LeeRoy rented it out."

"And it ruint the furniture," exclaimed Merle, "did LeeRoy make it right?"

"Well, in a word, no," said Doc. "He said there was nothing wrong with the unit, and that the furniture must have been soaking wet when they stored it, and that they were just trying to get him to pay for their new bedroom suite." Doc shook his head, "and I know that's not the case, because they had asked to use my truck, and I helped load and unload it. I told him so, but he flat refused to even talk about it. Then he told her to get her stuff out and don't bother him about it again. So we spent most of the night before last moving furniture – emptied it out just before midnight. "

"So what's that got to do with Jasper smelling like a… oh no! He didn't!' exclaimed Mattie.

"Yes, I'm afraid he did," chuckled Doc, "he came around late last night and woke me up and asked if I knew if a bottle of whiskey would calm a den of skunks so he could get them into a bag without getting sprayed. I told him I didn't have any idea, and asked him why in heck he was waking me up at that hour with such a foolish question, but he just mumbled something I couldn't understand, and left." He took a big swig of his coffee, and started refilling his pipe.

"So what happened?" asked Mattie, "I need to get back to the counter!"

"Well, I couldn't sleep, so I got dressed and followed after him."

"Walking?

"Yes, walking," said Doc. "He was headed into the woods down behind the Farley place, and he was carrying a jug, and that big old electric lantern of his, so he was easy to spot. And it was plain he'd already been into the jug a ways. So I followed. He was just stumbling along mostly, so it was easy to catch up with him, but I didn't want to spook him so I stayed back to watch. Sure enough, he knew where there was a den of skunks, a momma and three or four kits, and he stopped right over it and uncorked the jug. I watched him sprinkle some in the hole, and then take a sip himself. Then he'd sprinkle some more, and sip some more. Pretty soon he got a good rhythm going – sprinkle, sip, sprinkle, sip, until he was at the bottom of the jug. I guess he figured it was as good a time as any, so he got a rucksack out of his pocket, and made a grab into the hole. I have to hand it to him – he got the whole skunk family into that bag before he gave up and started heaving up what he'd drunk of that whiskey! Then after a few minutes he picked up the sack and started over towards LeeRoy's storage sheds. And I went home to get a couple hours' sleep."

Mattie looked like to bust a gusset. "And that's why LeeRoy sent Doo in for the coffee this morning. He must have opened that shed to clean it out for the next customer, and got sprayed!"

"Likely," said Doc, "most likely…"

The End

Jump Start

"Brrrrr! It's cold out there!" Doc brushed the snow off his hat as he came in the front door of the diner.

Harlow followed close behind, stomping snow off his boots, and started in to cussing at the weather. "Blankety blank colder than a wi…"

"Never mind that kind of talk, Harlow Tibbets! We don't need that in here!" Mattie glared at the offending truck driver, then nodded a welcome to Doc. "Yeah, Charlie had to come over and jump start the Ford this morning or I wouldn't have got here in time to open!"

Marie came out of the kitchen, still nervous over being a few minutes late on only her third day on her new waitressing job. She poured Harley a coffee, then went over to where Doc and Mattie were conversing. "What's 'jump-starting'?"

Doc looked at Mattie and grinned. "Ahh youngsters! Missed all the good stuff that we had so much fun doing!"

"Or inventing," agreed Mattie. "Go ahead, Doc, *you* explain it to her!"

Doc helped himself to coffee and a cheese Danish, and established himself in his customary seat in the booth at the end of the counter, bringing the pot with him as usual. "Well, Marie," he chuckled, "jump-starting is slang for what you do to a car when the battery is drained and it won't start. Nowadays most folks agree that you need jumper cables to jump-start a vehicle, but cables weren't always necessary.

"According to the old-timers," he said, winking at Mattie, "the term really originated with the old stick shift cars. When the battery died, you pushed the car to get it rolling, then jumped in, put it in second gear, and popped the clutch. That would usually get the engine running, and the part where you jump in is where they got the term jump-start. At least that's the way I heard it." He paused, took a sip of the hot coffee and a bite of the Danish, and nodded to Merve Whitehead, who had just stomped in out of the cold. "Grab a mug and set down, Merve, Got coffee right here. Just going over some of the prehistoric stuff we old dinosaurs used to do." He winked at Merve as if to let him in on an inside chuckle. "Jump-starting One-Oh-One, you might say."

"Oh yeah," Merve grinned back, "know it well. Thanks for the brew, Doc, sure need it this morning."

Doc nodded, and turned back to Marie. "'Course, things got complicated when they started making those automatic transmissions. There was no clutch to pop, and that made it more difficult, because you had to get the car up to about forty miles an hour in order for it to start, and that could lead to problems.

"Like the time when Cousin Lester (that was his real name -- Cousin was his first name and Lester was his last). Anyway, Cousin Lester borrowed Merve's old "49 Oldsmobile one evening and took *his* cousin Junie on a date…" Doc paused and turned to Merve, who had finally got himself warmed up – "Why don't *you* fill in the details, seeing as it was *your* car?"

Merve gulped down the rest of his first cup of coffee and held his mug out for a refill. "Ayyup", he said, "Cousin and Junie went out on a real date --movie and all -- and had themselves a real good time, until along about midnight. The car wouldn't start on account of he had left the radio on so they could set out front and listen to Elvis, and the battery died. There they were, out in the road in front of her house, and the car just would not start.

"Well, he told her that they would have to get another car to push the Olds, because it was hydramatic, and it had to get up to forty before it would start.

"So Junie said she'd just get her father's new Ford and jump-start the Olds. Cousin said okay, so Junie walked up the driveway, got in the Ford, and drove it down to the neighbor's barnyard to turn it around so she could come up from behind.

"Trouble was, she remembered that he'd said that it wouldn't work unless she got it up to forty..."

The End

Old Red Tiller

The November chill tried to follow the old farmer through the front door of Mattie's Place, but he managed to shut it out as he headed for the counter. "Hey, Calvin!" came the gruff, but pleasant voice from the end booth. "Come on over and set a spell. I need to ask you something. Just grab yourself a mug and come on over. I've got a fresh pot right here."

"Hey, Doc! Don't mind if I do!" Calvin settled in across from the chief denizen of Mattie's Place, and watched him pour a steaming mug of coffee, then freshen up his own. "What's up?"

"Well," replied Doc Howland, "we've got ourselves a couple of deer hunters with the heebie-jeebies." Cal just nursed his coffee and waited for Doc to continue. "Yep, Doug Harrigan and his brother-in-law Faye stopped in yesterday afternoon just after dark, and they were both acting nervous as all get-out. I asked what got their backs up so, and they came over and set right there, and proceeded to tell me about spooks up yonder – back of your picnic spot."

Calvin started to bristle at that, but Doc kept on talking. "I reminded them that you don't want anybody hunting on that part of your farm, and they said they knew that – they'd already unloaded their guns. They weren't hunting there, just taking a short cut along your fence line back from the state land, when they heard the drum."

The old man swallowed real quick at that, and acted still a little grumpy, but he allowed as how it was reasonable for them to be taking a short cut through there. "So what's this about drums?" He stared at the counter, and tried to act calm and natural, but Doc saw his hand shake as he picked up his mug again.

"Careful, Cal," said Doc quietly, so as not to attract attention. "Don't spill it on you. It's still pretty hot!" He looked closely at the old farmer, and continued, "They were already trying to think up a logical explanation for it, and had decided that it was maybe just a ruffed grouse down in the hollow. I told them that sounded about right. When the air is heavy it sort of muffles the thumping the grouse makes. But what I *didn't* tell them was that we haven't seen any ruffed grouse around here since Hector was a pup." He looked intently at Calvin, sensing that the old farmer had a story to tell. "None of my business, Cal, but it occurs to me that maybe *you've* heard Indian drums out there too."

Calvin glanced around the mostly empty diner, then looked back at Doc and said with a sigh, "Well maybe I have at that." He seemed relieved to be sharing something that had been on his mind for some time, and with someone he knew he could count on to keep it in strict confidence. He looked around to see if anyone else was close enough to overhear, then turned back to Doc. "And maybe you can tell me if I'm crazy or not." He smiled briefly – "Ruffed grouse? I don't know if I'd have thought of that one. Like you said – since Hector was a pup." He held out his mug for a refill, nodded his thanks, and began:

"Most of my friends know I love to garden, and I can't ever find enough room to plant some new variety of vegetables. So they sometimes ask me why, right in the middle of an obviously good garden spot, I have a big boulder, with a big, thorny, hawthorn tree planted next to it.

"I admit it looks a little strange at first, but I usually just say that I thought it would be a good place to sit and read or write, or to take a break from tilling and weeding.

It's a nice place to just watch the birds, or to plan on how to do in the critters and pests that won't leave my beans and potatoes alone – or just a place to sit and think, or chat with the Good Lord. But there's more to it than that, but I reckon you've guessed that already.

"It goes back to about twenty years ago, when I bought a used tiller. You know the kind, a great big red one with the tines on the rear. It was a 1963 model, already twenty years old, but still in great shape. I couldn't pass up the deal. I brought it home, cranked it up, and proceeded to till up a real nice spot for some fresh veggies, and even some flowers for my wife.

"As the years went by I used that tiller to expand my garden and grow even more stuff. I tried several different kinds of tomatoes, beans, squash, you name it, I had the gardening bug really bad, and that red tiller got lots of use.

"Then a couple of years ago I decided to till up a rough spot on one side of the garden, to see if I could improve the soil there, enough to raise some melons and sweet corn. The kids had used it for a play yard, but now it just grew up to weeds and briars, so I thought maybe at the very least I could smooth it out and grow some decent grass, if nothing else. So I filled up the gas tank, checked the oil, cranked up "Big Red," and started tilling.

"About halfway down the second pass the engine quit. 'Okay, it's old,' I thought to myself as I pulled on the starter rope. No luck. It turned over okay, but wouldn't start. So I mumbled a little, dragged the thing back to the edge of the garden, and checked everything over. Try again. I pulled on the rope and it started right up! "Must have been some dust," I thought, and went back to tilling.

"It ran great, back to that same spot, and stalled again! Same routine as before, it wouldn't start, no matter what I did, until I pulled it back to the edge of the garden. As soon as I did that, it started right up again and ran like a champ! I ran a few passes through the other garden just to make sure it was okay, then back over to the new spot. It stalled again, in the same place. This was getting spooky! I could hear the "Twilight Zone" theme in the back of my head!

"I put thoughts of Rod Serling out of my mind, and started scratching around in the spot where it had stalled. I thought there must have been a big rock or patch of heavy clay soil right there, and it just bogged down. I keep an old army surplus entrenching tool strapped to the handle of the tiller to dig out big stones if I hit them, so I got it out and started digging. There were the usual flat stones, and a cobble rock, but no clay. It was even a little sandier than where my main garden is.

"Then I found an arrowhead! I had found arrowheads in the garden before, so it wasn't really a surprise, but then I found another, along with a stone hand-axe and some beads. More points, and some shards of flint – and then I stopped. There was a larger rounded thing that looked at first like another cobblestone, but right away I knew it wasn't. I didn't have to dig any further to know that it was no stone at all. It was the former owner of the arrowheads and other stuff I'd already uncovered.

"I could hear more than theme music now. It was probably just the blood rushing in my ears, or my heart beating, but it sounded like tom-toms, and I could swear I heard chanting in the distance. Part of me wanted to dig up the rest of the spot, but the sounds in my head and heart kept whispering 'No! Cover him back up and leave him be!!' So I smoothed it over as best I could, ran the tiller back to the barn and put it away. Didn't hardly dare to touch it.

"I couldn't bear to walk on the spot for a time, and it grew up to coarse weeds that I didn't even dare mow. But eventually I got around to thinking it might be nice to mark the spot with something more permanent. So I mowed it and re-seeded the bare spots. Then I took the tractor down by the old creek bed where I knew there was a big rough boulder. I wrestled it onto a skid, and dragged it back and placed it just so. Then I thought a big bushy hawthorn tree would look really nice there too. Some folks say there's something magical and mystical about hawthorns, so it seemed right. The thorns would give him some protection as well, so I found one and transplanted it. And oh, those thorns! It so happens that blood is a good fertilizer, and I guess that's a good thing, because I gave up some in that little chore!

"But now it's done, and it looks real nice. I put a bench nearby, and scattered some wildflower seeds around, and I keep the rest of it mowed so we can sit there and just watch the critters playing in the tree. It's real pretty, and it's become our favorite summertime spot to sit and relax. My wife says she can't hear the chanting, or the tom-toms, but I know she does, sometimes – just won't admit it. I do, sometimes, and I guess they sound approving.

"The tiller still runs, but I don't use it much. It's more a curiosity now, and has its own spot in the barn. I cleaned it up and repainted it last year. There's been a few people offered to buy it, but I can't sell it. I pull it out of the barn now and again, set the choke and pull on the starter rope, and that old engine still fires right up."

Calvin looked at Doc, who appeared lost in thought. "Doc?"

"Yeah, Cal?"

"Got any idea why that tiller would run anywhere but in that particular spot?"

"I've an idea, Calvin, but I'm not sure it fits in with anything I've ever seen before."

"You know what kind of engine is on that tiller, don't you, Doc?

"Yes, I believe I do, Cal. It's a Tecumseh, isn't it? Named for the Shawnee chief who said he'd protect his people forever?"

"Yes it is, Doc," Calvin took another long swig of coffee, "that faithful old Tecumseh engine…"

The End

Maybe Soon

"There – I think that got it okay, Bump. Thank goodness there're no leaks!" Doc put away the hair dryer he'd just used to thaw out the water pipe in Mattie's back room, and headed for the coffee pot.

"Thanks, Doc," called Mattie – "I owe you a breakfast!"

"You're welcome, ma'am. Over easy and home fries this morning, I think. Did the paper come yet? Or are they froze up too?"

"Here he comes now, Doc, and he looks chilled to the bone! Want to pour him a mug while I get these eggs started?"

The bell on Mattie's front door gave out its jangle, but even that sounded cold, as Big Jim came in and stomped his feet. "Wow!" he exclaimed. "That snow stings when it hits! Must be down near zero this morning." He dropped the morning papers on the counter and turned to hang his jacket on the hook by the door.

"Yeah," agreed Doc Howland, "just got that pesky water pipe thawed out again. You have trouble starting the Jeep this morning?"

"Not much, Doc. Oh, thanks, I needed that." He took a swallow of the steaming brew Doc handed him. "Yeah, I definitely needed that!"

"Almost done for the morning?" asked Mattie, as she brought him a warm blueberry muffin.

"Almost," said Jim, "just one more stop at the nursing home, and then I can get back to the house and tend to my own chores."

"Nursing home?" Doc motioned Jim to join him. Didn't your uncle pass away a couple of weeks ago?"

"Yeah, he did," replied the big man, his voice now softer. "But there's someone else up there now." He stared into his coffee for a minute, and his eyes grew sad and shiny. "Someone else now."

Mattie joined them, saying nothing as she saw the look on the big man's face.

Jim continued. "I was up to see Uncle Bryce just before he passed on, thinking that I probably wouldn't see the inside of 'The Maples' again for a long while. We had a nice visit, but he couldn't talk much, so I didn't stay long. As I came back out I saw old Hannah sitting in her usual spot near the aide's station. I just smiled at her like always, and started toward the door.

"She clutched at my hand as I started past her chair.

'Hello son, where have you been?'

"It surprised me, 'cause she'd never said anything to me before, so I answered with the first thing that popped into my mind: 'Out mowing the lawn.' I hoped she wouldn't realize there was still snow on the ground.

"Her cold hands caressed my own and drew them to her cheek. 'Did you trim around Dad's headstone?'

"I saw that faraway look in her eyes, and it about broke my heart. 'Sure did. He'll like it just fine.'

'I know he will. I just wish he'd come and take me away from here.'

"I glanced up at the aides standing nearby, and saw one had tears in her eyes and was slowly shaking her head.

'Maybe he will soon, maybe he will.' My throat was tightening, too.

"She smiled again. 'That's good. Maybe soon he'll come find me.'

"I kissed her forehead and got back up from where I'd knelt beside her chair, and left her smiling in the warm sunshine by his stone. As I turned away I heard her whisper again, 'Maybe soon.'

"One of the aides came and hugged me, and said 'It's been months since anyone in her family visited.'

"So now I've got another mom, at least until maybe soon."

The End

Our town is much like any other town, mostly pretty much predictable. But sometimes some pretty unexplainable things do happen, even to pretty explainable folks. Like the other evening, for example ...

An Old Hymn

"Just as I am, without one plea..."

The words and melody of the beloved old hymn ran through Tom Manning's mind as he walked quietly into the dimly lit sanctuary. He'd only been pastor here a month, but already he was beginning to love this old town, and this church with its dark paneling and tall stained glass windows. A late night visit to the sanctuary for prayer had quickly become a habit. The stillness did wonders to release the pressures of the day, and he felt closer to the Spirit that had called him to a life of service.

"But that thy blood was shed for me..."

"I love that old hymn," he thought, as he walked toward the altar. The music was soothing, almost hypnotic, and the tones of the old organ seemed to draw him closer to something wonderful, something that he couldn't quite put his finger on, but something that nagged at the corners of his mind as being out of place.

"And that thou biddest me come to thee..."

Wait! He realized suddenly that the music was not just in his mind, it really was coming from the pipes of the old organ in the chancel of the church. He hesitated, then quickened his steps toward the altar, and his gaze was drawn to the organ console, where he saw an old, white-haired man seated at the ancient keys.

"O Lamb of God, I come, I come…"

"Sir" Who are you? And please, how did you get in here?"

The old man looked up at him and smiled. "Hello, I'm Charles Borning, and I've come to repair this old organ."

"Repair the organ?" Tom was confused. "But they said that it was beyond repair. It hasn't been used for years! And we were just about to remove it and replace it with a new instrument" said the pastor.

"I know. That's why I was sent to repair it," smiled the old man. "I built it, you know. It's some of my best work, except for this old valve that I've just replaced."

"You *built* it?" said Tom.

"Well, yes, building these organs was my gift. They've pleased a lot of people, even brought comfort to some."

"But I don't understand. Who called you? Who authorized the work? We're a small church, and we don't have the money to pay for expensive repairs."

"No one called me; you might say I was sent. And you can call this warranty work. There's no charge; it's covered under the guarantee. I'm almost finished here now, and I must be going soon."

Thoroughly perplexed, Pastor Tom said "But wait, I still don't understand! Won't you stay for a minute? I was just about to have a cup of tea. Would you stay and have one too, and chat a bit?"

"Well, a cup of tea *would* be nice, at that. Working on this dusty old keyboard makes a body thirsty." The old man's eyes sparkled, and he smiled. "Yes, tea would be nice, thank you!"

"It won't take but a moment, sir," said Tom, "I'll bring it right out. He almost ran to his study, still wondering as he went. There was something familiar about the old man's name. He'd seen it somewhere, and just recently too. "I'll have to ask him," he thought, as he carried the tea tray back out to the nave.

"Here it is" he called, as he approached the organ. "Would you like milk, or sug ..." he stopped, looking around. The old man was gone. "Mister Borning? Where are you?" he called. There was no answer. He set the tray down, and touched the keys of the organ. Pure, sweet tones filled the sanctuary, but the old man did not come back.

As if in a dream he took the tray back to his study, and sat there in thought for several minutes, then left by the side door and walked past the old cemetery to his parking spot next to the church. The full moon illuminated his way as he walked to his car and got in, still thinking and wondering about the old man. He thought and prayed out loud "God, am I just dreaming this, or am I losing my mind?"

He opened his eyes, started the car, and turned on the headlights. Then he sat there and stared. There in front of him was the headstone he'd seen every day on his arrival at church. The inscription was simple:

Charles Borning
Organ Maker
1866-1951
"O Lamb of God, I Come"

For Our Country

The bell on the front door clattered as Doc Howland entered Mattie's place. "That new flag looks good out there, Mattie," he said, as he headed for his favorite booth at the end of the counter.

Mattie closed the register and wished Charlie a good day, then turned and grabbed the coffee pot and headed in his direction. "Thanks Doc," she said, as she poured his first cup of coffee. "The old one was getting a little ragged, and it just didn't seem right to fly it on Veteran's Day. I know too many vets who fought to keep it flying, and it would be a shame to fly an old beat up flag, especially today. And by the way, coffee's on me today for all vets."

"And we appreciate it, Mattie," said the big man at the counter." I just wish some of my old buddies were here to take you up on it. Carl, especially, would have appreciated seeing that flag flying."

"Who's that, Jim?" asked Doc, "I never heard you mention him before. Is he from around here?"

"No," said Jim, "he wasn't from here at all, and I only got to know him for a little while." The big man's voice cracked a little, and he looked down and stared at his coffee for a minute, and Mattie thought she saw his eyes well up.

Jim regained his composure, and looked back up and smiled, but his eyes were still shiny. "Carl was a guy I knew in the service. You'd loved him if you ever met him. He wasn't from around here at all, but he loved everything about here."

Doc studied Jim for a minute, and said "Sounds like someone real special. Where'd you get to know him?"

"Well, I never told anyone but Ellen much about Carl, and she tried to contact his family for me before she died, but never could find them. I guess maybe now I do need to let folks know who he was," said Jim. He moved closer to where Doc and Mattie sat. Others at the counter, not used to hearing Jim say much at all, started to pay attention too. Jim took a swallow of coffee, and began his story.

"His name was Carl Voigt, and I first met him in September of 1963, on a recruit transfer bus at Fort Dix, New Jersey. We were both trying to understand all the shouting and cursing that we could hear all around us. I don't know that we ever really did make sense of it, but we heard it a lot during the eight weeks we spent together. And we were both trying our best to drag and carry those gawd-awful duffel bags! They were full of everything the Army told us we'd need for the next eight weeks. It was confusing and frustrating for me, but even harder for him because he didn't have much English yet. I thought he could speak it pretty well, but he tried to hide his German accent.

"We were about the same age - a couple of years older than most of our basic training company. I had fooled around in a couple of jobs after high school, and had joined the Army for lack of something better to do. Carl had spent that same time coming to America to find a place to live, to live a dream. He was hopelessly convinced that America was his "promised land," a place where he could be anything he wanted to be. So he came and learned, and worked, and saved, and applied for citizenship.

"And got drafted.

"Drafted!

"I had enlisted mostly because I was bored, but he had actually *volunteered* for the draft, to be a part of what I had taken for granted. It didn't seem fair, somehow, but he was happy about it. He said that it would give him a chance to learn more about our country. Already he was calling it "Our Country." "He sounded proud of it every time he said it. And he took it seriously when JFK said 'Ask not …'

"Carl was one of the most good-natured men I ever met. He had to be, what with all the flak he had to take for being also one of the slowest and clumsiest guys I ever met. Not so much slow, I guess, more like deliberate. He wanted to get it right. He usually did.

"We were about as evenly matched as anybody could be, and we got to spend a lot of time together. Push-ups, KP, gas mask training, hand-to-hand, bayonet drills, mud, dust, you name it, we ended up in the middle of it. About halfway through the training cycle we were bending over puking up our guts after gas mask training, and I asked Carl why he put up with it - he could have quit it any time he wanted to, and still gone on for his citizenship. And he smiled, and said "For our country. For our country I want to do this."

"We were training on the bayonet range the day that President Kennedy was assassinated. I stood next to him when they told us, and the tears ran down his cheeks just as they did mine. We went to the Regimental Chapel that night - we spent a lot of our spare time there - and prayed for "Our country."

"Something changed in him that day. Something changed in all of us, I think, but especially in him. He got quieter, more determined to do something good, to make up for the atrocity in Dallas.

"In the next few days we finished rifle training, the grenade range, and the infiltration course, and it was all I could do to keep up with him. Then we graduated from basic training. My folks drove down for it. I introduced them to Carl, and they invited him to come and stay with them any time. He appreciated that, and said he would, as soon as he got the chance.

"Well, I had orders cut for signal school. Eight months of technical training, then an easy assignment in Germany. He laughed at that - I was going to be stationed near where he had grown up! He, on the other hand, was headed for Advanced Infantry Training - another eight weeks of the same kind of hell we'd just completed. He just shrugged it off. "For our country" was the mantra we'd gotten used to hearing from him, and his acceptance of it didn't surprise us.

"We said goodbye at the end of November, and promised to keep in touch. I told him he'd have to take leave and come see me in Germany, but he said no, he wanted to see more of America. He even wanted to stop to see my folks! He gave me a bear hug and said goodbye, and several of the other guys made their good-byes in the same way. Then I got on the bus for Fort Monmouth, and he picked up his duffel bag, slung it over his shoulder. He carried it a lot easier than the first time I saw him, and he headed off to his new barracks.

"The eight months at signal school went by quickly. I got my orders to Germany, and headed back to Fort Dix to wait at the replacement station for the next troop ship. I had a few days there with not much to do, so I wandered back to the old Echo Company barracks to see if any of the cadre were still there. Our platoon sergeant was gone, but the company clerk and a couple of the other NCOs were in the orderly room when I walked in.

"Wiggins, the clerk, remembered me from chapel. He used to sit with Carl and me so we could sing harmony together. We got to BS-ing about different things that had happened in our training cycle. We laughed over the rain and mud we got into on bivouac, and how Carl and I ended up eating seconds and thirds of the liver and onions they brought out to us.

"Wiggins stopped laughing then, and I looked at

him and saw the look in his eyes. And I knew. 'Oh God, don't let him say what I know he's going to say...'

"Carl had finished AIT, and had shipped out to Vietnam a few days after that. No muss, no fuss, just sayonara, sucker, and don't bother to write. Wiggins was sketchy on the details, but one of the other guys who got shipped out with Carl had written to say that a week after they landed and were sent up country, there had been a mortar attack on their compound, killing three of our guys. Carl was one of them."

Jim's voice trailed off for a minute, and they could see he was struggling to keep from crying. Mattie put her hand on his shoulder, and he nodded and went on in a whisper. "'For our country,' he would have said with that gentle smile – 'for Our Country.' "

Jim's voice got stronger again, and sounded angry for a moment. "Sometimes I get angry when I think about the guys who headed north of the border, just to get out of doing their duty. I always get real angry when I think about how a lot of the guys who made it home from 'Nam got treated."

He took a breath, and let it out slowly. "But somehow I think that Carl wouldn't have let it bother him. He wasn't so concerned about what other people did, as long as he could do something 'For our country.'"

The diner was quiet for a time after he finished his story, and a couple of the older hard-bitten farmers pulled out handkerchiefs and blew their noses.

Mattie bit her lip and looked out the window, at the Stars and Stripes flying proudly in the morning sun. She rubbed her eyes, and was quiet for a minute, and then she whispered "Thank you, Carl."

The End

Myrna

"What the heck happened to *you* !?"

Everyone in the diner turned to see who Mattie was hollering at, and there in the doorway stood a skinny little guy, looking like last place in a butt-kicking contest.

"I'm okay," he mumbled, "just need some coffee." He squinted around the diner, having difficulty seeing through a swollen left eye, and past an obviously broken nose.

"Somebody get him a chair" hollered Merle, 'before he falls down!"

Doc shook his head and said "No, Merle, just help him over here so I can take a look at him."

Merle did as he was told, and soon the young man was safely stowed away in the corner booth, Doc Howland's private domain. Leastwise, that's how all the regulars treated it. Everybody knows "That's where *Doc* sets, and don't forget it!"

"What in thunderation *did* happen to you? Your face looks like you French-kissed Alice Chalmers!" Merle stood there, obviously pleased with his little jest, even though he wasn't exactly sure what it meant, and he was as curious as all get-out.

The guy tried to grin, but it came out a little lop-sided, and it was plain to see that the effort was painful. He settled for shaking his head and looking around for the coffee Mattie had just set on the table beside him.

Doc gave Merle that "Button-your-lip-and-get-out-of-the-way," stare, and Merle shut up and moved to the next booth, still hanging on every word. Doc got out that little flashlight he carries and shined it at the battered face in front of him, trying to see the extent of the damage. "For your information, Merle, this young worthy is Jimmie Hanford. He bought the Doolittle place over on Mount Hunger a couple months ago. I've known him since he was a young'un – went to school with his Pa, over in Tioga County." He turned back to the young man. "What happened, Jimmie?" He gently touched a swollen spot near the corner of Jimmie's eye and said "Cheek bone looks okay, but that nose will never be the same. You should get X-rays. Was it Myrna again?"

Jimmie winced and pulled back, just as Mattie arrived again, this time with a handful of ice from the cooler, wrapped in a kitchen towel. He nodded his thanks, and put the ice against the side of his face. Then he turned back and nodded to Doc. "Uhuh. Myrna again."

Doc shook his head. "Didn't I tell you she's pure poison? No way a man ought to put up with an attitude like hers. Last time she broke your ribs, and before that it was a concussion. What'd she hit you with this time?"

"Didn't hit me with anything, Doc," mumbled Jimmie, "she up and *kicked* me when I was looking the other way."

"*Kicked* you?" broke in Merle, "If *my* old lady ever done that to me it'd be all day for her!"

"Merle?" said Mattie.

"I would've slapped her so silly she'd think it was Tuesday!"

"Merle!" (a bit louder this time)

"I'd have had the sheriff lock her up till she's 90! Teach her a less…"

"MERLE!" hollered about half the denizens of Mattie's Diner.

Doc and Jimmie just looked at him and Doc shook his head. "In the first place, you're not even married, so what do you know about it?"

"But if I was..."

"And in the second place, the way you keep flapping your pie-hole you're not likely to *ever* get married!"

Merle began to get the idea that he was well into one of Doc's famous lectures. "But, but..."

"But me no buts, you poor unenlightened excuse for an ignoramus!" (Merle hated it when Doc used them big words) "In the *third* place, Jimmie's not married either!"

"He's not? Then wha...? Then who's Myrna?"

"Myrna just happens to be a little bit feisty, but she's the best dang Guernsey in the county. And everybody knows, except maybe you, that in order to get the most out of a Guernsey you have to finish milking her by hand. And Jimmie, here, happens to have just about the coldest pair of hands in the county!" He paused, looked at Jimmie, and grinned. "Which, come to think of it, is maybe why *he* doesn't have a wife *either*!"

The End

Officer Barney and the Deer Hunters

They call him "JB," but his name tag only has his last name – "Barney." And no, don't start thinking Mayberry or purple dinosaurs, 'cause it won't get you any points with him. He's heard it all, seen it all, and he's "been there, done that."

Well, he *thought* he'd seen it all until last week – the first day of deer season in these parts.

JB came into Mattie's Place the other day, for his usual Tuesday morning biscuits and gravy. He's starting to take a liking to them, even though he couldn't stand them at first. He'd just ordered them because he was so taken by the new waitress – Marie – that all he could think of was what she'd just put in front of Clayton, and he got so tongue-tied that he ordered them before even thinking. It's strange how she has that effect on near everybody. But now everybody knows she's JB's gal, and everybody's happy about that, 'cause they seem to "fit together walkin'," like the song says.

Marie was taking her break, sitting with Doc in his booth, and she waved JB over to join them. "Sure," grumbled Doc, good-naturedly, "just when I get a chance to set a spell with the prettiest girl in town, in comes the law, and I have to take the back seat again." The twinkle in his eye belied the grump in his voice as he welcomed the deputy to a seat in the booth. "Like some coffee, JB?"

JB slid in next to Marie, and said "You know I do, Doc, and today I think I need it." He rubbed his eyes and shook his head, as if to clear the cobwebs. He swallowed a big mouthful of Mattie's finest, and said "Yep, I needed that."

Marie, sensing something was amiss, asked JB if he was okay. He just looked at her with a bemused expression on his face, and assured her that he was fine, just trying to keep from busting out laughing over what he'd just seen.

Of course this got Doc's attention, and he poured JB some more coffee, as Mattie delivered the biscuits. "*Now* what's up, JB" she asked, "did one of our great white hunters shoot himself in the foot?"

JB shook his head. "No, nothing like that," he said, and he started to chuckle. "It was just a couple of city kids, come up to impress us "hicks" with their hunting skills."

"Them doggone city 'hunters,'" sputtered Merle, who had been listening in as usual. "I remember one…" he broke off, embarrassed at having interrupted again. "Sorry," he mumbled, "I done it again."

"Anyway," JB continued, used to Merle's interjections, "I was out on the ridge road, just cruising and looking for road hunters, when I met a couple of young fellas driving a big Buick. I could tell from the plates that they were from downstate, but that's not why I stopped them." He paused, took another sip of coffee, and looked at Merle to make sure that worthy didn't interpret the pause as an invitation to impart some of his own insights. Merle had his mouth half open, but switched his attention to the bottom of his mug. So the deputy continued.

"Well, I walked up to the car and said howdy to the two individuals in it. I invited them to get out and talk for a spell. Asked 'em if I could take a look at their licenses, check their deer tags, and all that." He started to chuckle again at that, and Marie gave him a playful swat, reminding him that her break was about over, and she wanted to hear the end of this.

"Okay!" he said, still laughing, "Don't get your undies in a bunch! It's hard enough telling this with a straight face.

I still can't believe it myself! I've been a deputy long enough that I thought I'd …"

Mattie broke in this time. "Will you get to it, *Barney? I'd* like to hear the rest of it before I get too much older, too!"

"Okay, okay!" He took another sip, regained his composure, and continued. "Well, I begun by explaining to them about how they hadn't ought to be carrying deer rifles in shotgun country, especially *loaded* deer rifles, in the car and all, and I wrote 'em up a ticket for that. Then the ticket for violating the open container law, It didn't matter that they weren't drunk or anything like that, just having the open cans of beer in the cup holders was enough.

"Then I told them I'd just give them a warning on the busted tail light lens, but they'd better get it fixed as soon as they could. And neither of them was using a seat belt. The belts were both shoved around back of the seat, so I had to write that one up as well." By this time the deputy was obviously trying to keep from laughing out loud, and Mattie and Marie were both trying to hold their tempers. He caught their expressions and sobered up.

"But the real kicker… hey Doc," he said, "remember a couple months ago when old man Merkle was complaining about how his wife was trying to get him to get rid of that old billy goat of theirs?"

Doc nodded, and looked a little confused at the change in subject. "Yeah, I remember," he said, "Clive said his wife got upset when the goat got into the blackberries, so she wanted it got rid of, but old softie Merkle couldn't do it. We picked on him someth…" He stopped in mid sentence as it dawned on him, and just looked at JB incredulously. "Really?"

JB ignored the exasperated sputtering from the rest of the group, and grinned. "Yep, I allowed as how it looked as if they'd had some luck after their trip up from the city.

"They puffed up like two banty roosters, and pleased as punch they said that yes, they'd got a nice spike horn, and they made sure they tagged it all legal and proper, and I could check it if I wanted. The one even asked if it might be a new state record for a spike horn buck.

"I felt bad about making them follow me back to Merkle's place, and even worse about him and his wife laughing so hard when they saw that old billygoat, hog-dressed and tied across the front fender of that Buick, but what could I do?"

The end

Road Rage

They were talking about road rage in the diner the other day, and about how bad it gets during construction season, what with all those orange and white cones along the road. Most of us are looking forward to seeing them disappear forever, or at least for the winter, which around here only seems like forever. Anyway, a couple of them did just that one morning late in the season, and to hear him tell it, we almost lost one of our regulars to boot …

Everybody at Mattie's Place jumped at the sound of screeching tires, followed by the blaring horn. They winced in anticipation of the sound of crunching metal, but gave a collective sigh of relief when it didn't come. A few minutes later, Fernal Owens came in, looking a little pale. He headed over to the counter and grumbled "Coffee, Marie – black."

"Sure, Fernal," replied the waitress, as she glanced out the window toward Fernal's Chevy Nova. She winked at Doc Howland, sitting in his customary booth at the end of the counter, and turned back to Fernal. "Directional signals not working again?"

"Yes, they're working, and yes, I used 'em!" The old farmer sounded disgusted. "Drivers nowadays got no patience at all. No regard for anyone else on the road." He took a seat at the end of the counter and looked over at

Doc. "And that's the *second* close call I've had today. It's enough to make a man go back to walking!"

"Second time?" asked Doc. "No *wonder* you're testy! What happened?"

"Well," said Fernal, "I was headed south on the interstate this morning, and everything was fine and dandy until I got to the construction signs, and all them traffic cones. They got the *left* lane closed now, and they give you 1500 feet to get over, and slow down to 40. Of course, that don't apply to *everybody*," he continued sarcastically, "at least not to Freightliners, rednecks, and big, expensive Lincolns. But they do give you time to slow down and get ready for it."

Doc lit up his pipe, nodding sympathetically. "Sounds about normal so far," he said, "so then what?"

"Well, being a law-abiding type, I figured I was okay with all that, and it would be just another case of looking in the rear-view mirror and seeing the white knuckles on the steering wheel behind me. Usually I can see them real good because nobody likes to slow down to forty anywhere, and I do it mostly just to see the reaction of the guy on my bumper. Sometimes they get close enough to where you can look back and see the veins on their foreheads standing out." At the thought of this, Fernal grinned, and looked around for Marie, and the coffee pot. She was headed that way, still listening, so he continued.

"Anyway, I was ready for the big, mostly-red van that had dibs on the one lane ahead. I won't mention any names – I think you know who I mean, and I knew he was going to take the lead, come hell or high water. And sure enough there he went, almost too fast for me to read that new sign on the side of his van:

LESTERS ANIMAL HOSPITAL AND
TAXIDERMEY SHOPPE,

and on the back it said:

IETHER WAY YOU
GET YOUR DOG BACK.

Doc smiled and said "Yep, I know exactly who you mean. I think Charlene made the sign. She answered one of those '*Make Money Making and Selling Magnetic Signs!*' ads. Her spelling is atrocious, and Lester's just not the type to be putting the extra PE on SHOPPE, if you know what I mean."

Fernal nodded, took another gulp of coffee and held out his mug for another refill, then looked at Merle, who was hanging on every word. "Exactly. And you're right, her spelling's atrocious! Anyway, Lester made it through okay, but a few car lengths back, and getting bigger by the second, was little old white-haired Missus Huckabee in that Nimitz-class Lincoln o' hers. She was coming on like there was no tomorrow. I mean she was moving like she'd been on her third cup of coffee when she remembered she was out of watertight undies! Well, you get the idea."

There was a snorting, strangling sort of gasp from the end of the counter as Clifford, always interested in a good story, tried to swallow the gulp of hot coffee he'd just taken. Marie frowned, and headed his way with her mop-up towel.

Fernal looked over that way, and waited for the interruption to die down. "Anyway, behind *her* was a big yellow and white J.B. Hunt Freightliner, and he must have had the governor about to blow out – he was moving that fast!

"I was into the narrows by then, so I couldn't do too much except hold my ground, what with Vern fishtailing up ahead, and old JB gaining on all of us. So I just hung on and started singing "Lord I'm Coming Home" real loud. Then she must have hit the brakes, because as I looked back to see where she was, I saw the Lincoln's bumper dip real low, (looked like the cow-catcher on old '97) and the left front brake must be pulling, cause it jigged over that way. If you see Sid before I do, tell him he ought to check it, next time she stops in. Anyway, she pulled far enough to the left so that she scooped up a couple of those orange and white traffic cones. Now that was *impressive*!

"I mean, them cones went for a ride! Even old JB slowed down to watch! One of 'em spiraled off into the brush like a wounded goose, and the other ricocheted off a northbound Peterbilt. I don't think they'll ever find the one, and the other wouldn't do 'em much good if they did."

I see some of them are real bunged up," offered Clifford, eager to become a real part of the conversation. "Just yesterday I was telling Wilm…" He lapsed into an embarrassed silence as he realized everyone else was glaring at him. "Sorry, Fernal," he mumbled.

Fernal nodded in exasperation. "Well *anyway,*" he continued, "she finally got that barge in a straight line behind me, and I could see in the mirror her jaw was going a mile a minute. Couldn't see anyone in the car with her, so I knew she was jawing at me! There wasn't much I could do at that point, so I just kept on the way I was going, and she kept real close behind me, and started blinking her lights as if she wanted me to run up on old Lester, who by this time had hit the binders to slow down and check out some road kill.

I ignored her for a quarter-mile or so, up to where we got back into two lanes. She saw it coming and started accelerating, way too soon for my heart rate, and timed it to within a bumper sticker! I mean, it's a good thing I didn't get the Nova repainted like I wanted to, because she never would have had room to pass if I had! As she went by, I just kind of shrugged, and held up four fingers to remind her that the limit through here was 40. That sweet little old lady never hesitated a bit, and signaled right back that she was gonna go at least one mile an hour faster!"

He grinned, took another swallow of coffee and held his mug out for a refill. Then he looked back over to Doc and grinned even wider, "At least, I *think* that's what she meant..."

The End

Solarium

"The Maples" sits in a pretty spot just on the edge of town, and some of our older folks consider it a comfortable resting place while they wait for that Heavenly Express to stop for them. Not that they've given up, mind you, but some of them prefer each other's company to the hustle and bustle found even in a small town like ours. Some of them even provide their own company. Like on a warm spring morning a few days ago ...

"Are you asleep, Goodman?"

"I was until now, but I guess not any more."

"How are you this morning?"

"*How are you this morning*? Always 'how are you this morning!' What do you care how are you this morning? I don't even know what day it is and you want to know how are you this morning. It could be yesterday still, or even tomorrow. What makes you so sure it's this morning? Hah?"

"I just wanted to be pleasant, and make some conversation to pass the time."

"Pass the time? What pass the time? Pass *away* would be pleasant!"

"You know and I know that you don't mean that, Goodman."

"Well maybe someday I will, maybe someday."

"That's good, then I guess I don't have to worry. If you don't know if it's today, how are you going to know when it's maybe someday?"

"Hmphh."

"Goodman?"

"What now?"

"Did you hear Roy Rogers died?"

"Who?"

"Roy Rogers. Dead. He was 83. "

"I'm 83"

"So?"

"I'm not dead."

"No, you're not dead."

"I'm 83."

"He didn't *die* from being 83. It was a heart attack, or something. Did you hear about it?"

"As a matter of fact, I did. You told me about it yesterday, or maybe it was today, since we don't even know what day it is. You'll probably tell me again tomorrow."

"Tell you what?"

"Roy Rogers is dead."

"I know he is, I told you that yesterday."

"Yes, you did. That Doody guy too, Buffalo Bill, whatever his name was."

"Bob. Buffalo Bob"

"That's him. Bob. Buffalo Bob… Dead."

"They're all going."

"Not going, dummy, gone. Burns, Sinatra, Riley. Now Roy Rogers. All gone."

"Riley?"

"Riley the crossing guard, the one on the corner. Gone."

"Yeah, Riley."

"All gone."

"Not many left any more."

"Even less, if you don't let me be...okay?"

"Okay."

"Okay."

"Say Goodman?"

"*Now* what?"

"Do you think she'll come by today?"

"Do I think *who'll* come by today?"

"You know who -- do you think she's coming by today?"

"How do *I* know 'is she coming by today?' You're the one who's goofy over her, mister order-me-some-flowers-for-my-case-worker! Goofy!"

"Never mind, it was for her birthday, and you're just jealous!"

"What jealous? She's too young for me – you too. Besides, she's got a hyphen."

"A hyphen?"

"A hyphen."

"What's a hyphen got to do with things? She's married!"

"In her *name* a hyphen, moron. You know, two last names, with a hyphen in the middle?"

"I told you, Goodman, women today are different."

"Hyphens."

"Anyway I like her big brown eyes."

"It was *your* eyes that were big, and it wasn't her *eyes* you were looking at!"

"You're crazy."

"I think I'll take a nap."

"Hyphens."

"Well *there* you are, Mister Goodman! I've been looking all over for you! Then someone said you've been here all alone in the solarium all morning. I do wish they wouldn't leave you in here all by yourself! I just came to thank you for the lovely flowers! How are you feeling today?"

"Not so good today, I think. Did you hear? Roy Rogers died..."

--

Tree house

Mattie's cousin Pat is an English teacher in the middle school in town. She stopped by a couple weeks ago for a blueberry muffin, and was telling Mattie how frustrating it was that her students simply would not take an interest in reading. National Reading Week was coming up fast, and she wanted to do something in her class to get the kids to pick up a book and read it. Mattie suggested that maybe Pat was too close to the problem, that someone else might be able to talk with the kids and encourage them in another way. About that time the door bell jangled. Mattie looked to see who was coming in, and said to Pat, "There you go, Jim's a writer! Maybe he'd do it!"

The big man looked puzzled. "Do what? Mattie, what're you getting me into now?" He gave them a good-natured smile, and said "Hi Pat! How's my favorite English teacher?"

"Oh, pretty good, I guess, except something's been bugging me, and we thought maybe *you* could help."

"We? Now you're ganging up on me?" Jim rolled his eyes in mock exasperation, then smiled. "Okay, I guess I'm outnumbered. What's the problem, and what is it that I can do to help?"

Well, that led to a discussion on the reading habits, or lack thereof, of "today's kids," and since Jim is of the mind that there's no skill more important than reading, he said he'd be more than happy to come in and have a chat with her class. Pat was overjoyed, and said she'd check to see when she could fit it into the schedule. But when the other

English teachers heard about it, they arranged an assembly in the auditorium for the whole junior high! So it's a good thing Jim loves kids, because when he got to the school a few days later, he got to "chat" with over a hundred of them!

A few of them knew him from church and Scouts, and some remembered him from Little League and the annual VFW picnic, but not many of them knew he was a writer. They all sat in respectful silence when he went to the stage after Pat introduced him. Their eyes got real big when he announced the title of his little talk, which he prefaced by saying "Some of the words and names will sound strange to you, but I'll guarantee that you'll be able to find them in your library, or even on your computer, if you're interested. Your teacher will give you a list of authors, titles, and some vocabulary words when you leave today."

He sat on a tall stool, got comfortable, waited for the kids to quiet their rustling, and began: "I'd like to tell you about the summer I swam the Panama Canal

"Of course, swimming the Panama Canal lengthwise on a Thursday afternoon wasn't as easy as diving into a sacred Mayan sacrificial well, but I still made it home in time for supper.

"I guess it was sometime during the middle of June; I never kept track of time back then, anyway. I didn't even own a watch until after high school, but I had a red-handled hammer, some bent nails, and some old barn boards, and I built the best tree house for miles around.

"I swapped a fingernail for some straightened sixteen-penny spikes, (yes, it hurt) and I used them to nail up the main beams for my castle. It was twenty feet up in a clump of maples, and I could see dragons from there.

"I could climb to it straight up, but the best way was by climbing up the big tree on the edge, and swinging into it on a hidden rope, like Tarzan showed me. It was fun to build, and exciting to get to, but the best thing about it was all the good friends that I met up there, and all the stories they told. Listen up, and I'll tell you about some of them.

"One of the first was a man named Ishmael, and I saw the white salt on his tanned skin, and smelled the sea on his ragged clothes. I shivered with excitement as he told me about his painted friend Quequeg, about a captain obsessed with a white whale, and about how, ship and all, they followed Captain Ahab and that whale to a watery grave.

"Thirteen I was, matey, and ready to go off to sea right then, but first there was a desert island, and I stopped to hear Robinson Crusoe's tale, and to help him hunt wild goats. I'll never forget the thrill of finding that footprint and realizing we were not alone. My castle became a fort that day, and the neighborhood never knew that they'd been saved from an attack by vicious cannibals.

"One afternoon Tom Swift and Lucky Terrell showed up together. Tom and I had grand adventures driving motorcycles across the country, and I was Lucky's wingman as we flew Spitfires across the English Channel, right into the teeth of the Luftwaffe. We beat them in the Battle of Britain, and went home heroes that night, and we stood proud as Mr. Churchill made his speech to thank us.

"There was a sign on my tree house that said "NO GIRLS," but Louisa May Alcot clambered in anyway, petticoats and all, and told me two wonderful stories about some girls and some boys that she knew. I got to know Meg and Nat and all the rest, and I was happy and sad and I felt at home with them.

Then, even less ladylike, Mary Shelley appeared, and told about that Doctor Frankenstein, and the creation that finally destroyed him. I remember feeling scared and sad at the same time about that, and wondered if the creature really knew who he was, and where he had come from. And he wasn't at all like those old Boris Karloff movies, either.

"Albert Payson Terhune visited for a while, and he introduced me to Lad, a Grand Champion Collie. Lad and I ran together through the woods and fields, and I loved him. I cried myself to sleep the night he died, and to this day I can't bring myself to give his name to just any old dog.

"I had more visitors, and one of my favorites was Zane Grey. He told the best stories ever, about a time when men were maybe a little more honorable and true than they are these days, and I remember thinking that I wanted to be as honest and steadfast as Warren Neale, and Wils Moore ... and Lassiter. He told about a country he loved, and he used simple words that made it come alive in a way I'll never forget. He told about the color of the hills at twilight, the hazy purple color of the sage, the sound of the wind keening through the aspens at the entrance to a hidden canyon, and the smell of the coffee and mesquite smoke from the campfire. All seemed real, and I can close my eyes and know them even now.

"One day he brought Mark Twain with him, and I heard about Tom and Becky, and Injun Joe, and Huck Finn ... and Jim. That was the first time I really thought about folks who I thought were different from me. I'd seen black folks, sure, but somehow Jim made me realize that there wasn't any real difference; not inside, where it counts. I wanted to help him to escape, and I think I even prayed for him and Huck on that raft. He had the same name as me, and that made him all the more real.

"Sometimes the people who came were very strange, like the quiet man with the wild eyes who talked about soma and feelies, and a new kind of world. He scared me, and I didn't really like him but I let him talk anyway, because Mr. Jefferson had told me that everyone should have a right to say what's on his mind. But I remember thinking that Mr. Huxley's mind must have been bent or something, and I didn't invite him back for a long time. Maybe his world was brave, but it surely was strange, and I wanted no part in it.

"As the summer grew older and the days got shorter I started to get a little anxious. It was going to be fall before I heard everyone's story, and there were so many to hear. The visitors began to crowd into my hideout until there was scarcely room to stretch out, and I spent more and more time there with them.

"Richard Halliburton told me about exploring Aztec cities and jumping into Mayan wells, and he's the one who really swam that canal, but he made the telling of it so real that I felt every dangerous mile.

"Then Dan Mannix almost talked me into running away and being a carny, a fire-eater and a sword-swallower. But there were other things I needed to do.

"George Orwell made me uneasy again, with his newspeak and Big Brother, until I realized that the world he talked about was years away, and I wouldn't have to worry about it for a long time.

"Then a man named John told me about One whose hands still bear the marks that prove His love for me, and I became His.

"All too quickly it was almost time for school again. One more race through the forest with Natty Bumpo and Chingachgook, and it was time to go, to be what everyone else wanted me to be. But I wouldn't give up my friends, not ever, and they won't let go of me.

"My tree house still stands -- a place of wonder -- fixed somewhere between Oz and Perelandra. I can find my way there from anywhere. I still go there often, and renew old friendships, and make new ones.

"It was there that Frodo and Samwise challenged the Dark Lord, and Theoden King died, and Aragorn's sword was made whole again. And its beams and branches went all blurry when that last Elvin ship but one, set sail from the Gray Havens.

"Its walls bore witness when a young Jewish girl named Anne made me promise that I would never hate anyone because of who they were, or were not.

"There, C.S. Lewis told me the story of Perelandra. Then, in the cool quietness of a Fall afternoon, he smiled through tears, as he spoke of his Joy.

"The bright glow of platted moonlight illumined the pages as Zenna Henderson taught me about the People who held Wonder in their hands.

"The stars above it beckoned brightly as Asimov, Bradbury, Clarke, and others shared their visions of the future.

"There was a grey, cold fog around it as H.M.S. Ulysses drove, engines full ahead, to her final resting place beneath the icy black waters of the North Sea.

And on the day of Dr. Seuss' funeral,
I saw from its window a teary-eyed cat,
and he carried a red and white striped top hat,
and his red bow tie drooped as he shuffled his feet,
in a sad, sad procession down Mulberry Street.

"There were many more, and they're all still there. All my old friends, and new ones too, still beckon, waiting to tell and retell their stories; because that is what they live to do.

"They've invited me to come and tell a story of my own, and I tell them I'm not ready yet, that I don't have a story worth the telling yet, but they seem insistent, eager for me to join them.

"And I've promised them, and myself, that someday soon I will do just that."

Pat stopped in again last Friday, to thank Mattie for her great idea, and Jim was just getting ready to leave. She thanked him again for coming to share his love for books with the kids. She said "I don't think the kids had heard of many of the names you told them about, not right then, at least. But I was talking to Mr. Crowell, our librarian, and he was amazed at some of the titles they're checking out these past few days!"

Jim just smiled, and said "All I did was to introduce them to some old friends, and *they* did all the work." He opened the door, and turned back; "And I thank *you,* too, Mattie!" He winked at Pat, and said "Be ready at seven tonight?"

Pat blushed and nodded, and walked him to the door. She waved goodbye, then turned to a wide-eyed Mattie, blushed even more brightly, and said "You've been picking on me for years, saying I'd grow up to be an old maid school teacher. Well maybe now you just might have had a hand in proving your own self wrong!"

Old Gator

Merle was adamant: "I say Flatiron Pool will be way too crowded. No way I'm tangling up my new fly line, fighting all those opening-day fishermen!"

"Yeah," agreed Sid, backed up by Arlo's nod, "them city folks will be stumbling all over each other just for a chance at that big old Brown Trout that's supposed to be in there."

"You don't think 'Old Gator' is really there, do ya?"

"Yeah, Merle," affirmed Sid, "I really do. He's really there, just laying back in the deep water, relaxing in his favorite spot. And one of these days ..."

The bell over Mattie's front door rang just then, and Doc came in, hung his sheepskin vest on its usual hook by the door, and made his way to his own relaxing spot, namely the corner booth at the end of Mattie's counter. He grabbed a mug and a pot of coffee on his way, then sat and leaned back, nodding to the boys at the counter. "What's everyone staring at Sid for?" he asked. "Fishing stories again?"

Merle and Arlo both started to say something, stopped and looked at each other, and started in again. "Whoa!" said Doc. I'll *never* get to hear it if you two loons keep butting in on each other!" He looked at Sid. "What's got these two all excited?"

"Well Doc, I was about to tell 'em about Old Gator, and how I think I can catch him, but I don't think they really believe he's there."

"And you do, Sid?" Doc waved the coffee pot at Sid's mug. "Refill?"

Sid held out his mug for a warm-up. "That's a roger on both questions, Doc, yes, I really do. But I've got to get going. Got a pile of work to finish today, so I can be down to Flatiron Pool tomorrow early, before all them city folks get it too stirred up to fish."

"Roger! Ten four and over, Cap'n!" Arlo sing-songed, while Merle snapped a salute in Sid's direction. They never tired of kidding the big guy about how he'd hung on to some of the stuff he'd learned in his 20 years as a mechanic in the Army. Good thing for them he was as easy-going as they come.

"Now Arlo," Sid shot right back, "I've told you a hundred times I was a Staff Sergeant, not a Captain." He chugged his coffee, waved at Doc, and headed out the door.

"He certainly does seem to have a fixation on that big trout," mused Doc, "I wonder if he'll ever really hook into it?"

"I don't know," said Arlo, "it would probably be a sight worth seeing, now, wouldn't it?" And he got a look on his face that said he'd just had an idea (he never did have too many original ones), and he began to concentrate on it. You could almost hear the wheels turning as he pondered something. "C'mon, Merle," he said, "I need your help with an idea," and they both paid their bills and left.

"Uh-oh," said Doc, "I've seen that look before. It's mostly harmless, but someone is in for a big surprise."

Mattie just shook her head, and said "I just hope nobody ends up with stitches, like last time."

"Yep, me too," chuckled Doc, "but boys will be boys, and all that."

Well, opening day came and went, and the next day it was all quiet in the diner when Doc came in laughing and shaking his head.

"Hi, Doc," called Mattie, "what's so funny, so early?"

"I take it none of the Izaak Waltons came in yesterday afternoon," replied Doc.

"No, it was so quiet all day that I almost closed early. I was hoping someone special would come in for supper, but I was out of luck for the day, I guess."

Doc grinned at her; "Someone special? Got a boyfriend I don't know about?"

She stuck her tongue out at him, and swatted him on the shoulder. "Get over to your corner like a good boy. I'll bring the pot over, soon as it's done. Eggs or oatmeal this morning?"

"Eggs and home fries, I guess, and maybe some of that scrapple, this morning."

Mattie wrinkled her nose at him. "Hughie ate up the rest of the scrapple yesterday afternoon. I don't know how you can eat that stuff, anyway. How about a couple of pork chops instead?"

"Sounds even better! I only eat that scrapple to remind myself how terrible it really is."

"Okay, but then you've got to tell me what you were laughing about when you came in."

"Deal!"

Doc grabbed a mug from the rack, filled it with that strong black coffee, and made his way to his corner booth, still chuckling over the things he'd seen last night. He'd just opened the morning paper, when Mattie came back from the kitchen and sat across from him. "Okay," she said, "now what's so funny?"

He made her wait until he'd finished the article he'd been reading about opening day. He laughed again, and said "Well, they *almost* got it right!"

"Got what right? What in the world went on, that it made the paper?"

"Well," said Doc, holding out his mug for a refill, "remember day before yesterday, when Sid was bragging about how he thought he'd be putting that 'Old Gator' legend to the test? And Arlo and Merle were picking on him about it? That's what made the paper this morning, in the 'Dave's Outdoors' column. Part of it did, anyway"

"You mean he finally caught that monster?" Mattie's eyes got wide. "He'll be impossible to be around now!"

"It wasn't quite like that," said Doc, "but I think that yes, he'll be impossible to be around for a while.'

Doc continued, "Remember Arlo was talking a while back about making a fortune selling Army and Navy surplus? He'd picked up a bunch of stuff at one of those military surplus auctions, and was going to open a store in the old Richfield Station, and get rich."

"Yeah, I remember that," said Mattie, "but what's that got to do with …"

"Well, he didn't do so well, and ended up with a pile of olive drab junk, moldering away in one of LeeRoy's storage sheds. He got an idea the other day, when they were picking on Sid, and got Merle to help with it. They were going to give Sid a real bit of excitement this time. Merle helped him dig through all that junk, until they found what he'd been looking for, a Navy surplus frogman outfit, complete with tank, mask, and wet suit."

"Frogman!" Mattie was incredulous. "Arlo can't hardly swim, let alone do frogman stuff!"

"Be that as it may," continued Doc, "he figured it couldn't be too hard, seeing as it wasn't exactly the ocean he'd be diving into.

"So, bright and early on opening day, he dressed up in that wet suit, after patching a couple of holes with duct tape. They filled up the tank over at the Sunoco Station so Sid wouldn't suspect anything, and off they went to Flatiron

Pool. They snuck around the back side of it, through the hedge behind the creamery ,,,"

"But that's posted," said Mattie, "no one's supposed to go in there!"

"Absolutely," said Doc, "that's why they figured nobody would be looking for them on that side, and they could hide in the trees that overhang the water.

"The plan was, Arlo would get into the water and hide in the branches, and Merle would watch for Sid to cast his line over that way, where he always said Old Gator hung out. Then when he saw Sid throw out over that way, he'd give Arlo the high sign, and Arlo would dive under, go deep so nobody would see him, and grab Sid's line and pull like the very devil!"

"Those bone heads!" What a dumb scheme!" Mattie said, "Hold that thought, and I'll be right back with your breakfast." She headed out to the kitchen, and came back with enough to feed an army. "Thought I'd join you. It's still slow, 'cause of opening day, and I'm due for a break anyway. Okay, let's hear the rest of it."

Doc cut up a pork chop, "Mmmmm! Just the way I like them!"

"I know," said Mattie, "how long have we been fixing them for you? Now on with the story, or you won't get any more!"

"Okay, okay," protested Doc, "you're a hard woman to deal with!" He grinned, and went on: "Anyway, Merle gave the high sign, pointed to where Sid had thrown his lure, and Arlo submerged, just like Lloyd Bridges in one of those old Sea Hunt episodes. Remember him? He used to ..."

"Doc! The rest of the story!"

He grinned and continued. "Okay, Arlo had a little trouble with the mask for a time, but got it cleared up, and ducked back under the water. He stuck close to the bottom, grabbing the rocks and stuff to haul himself along the way he wanted to go, and spotted Sid's spoon, dead ahead. He made a grab for it, which turned out to be a dumb thing to do, because he got a hook stuck in his thumb, and tried to yank his hand back.

"Well, Sid felt the tug on his line, and it felt like a monster had grabbed it! Boy, that really got his heart started! So he reared back and set the hook real good, which caused no end of distress to Arlo, who by this time was thinking only of getting out of there!

"Sid thought he'd got ahold of Old Gator, and he let out a holler, and started fighting this critter on the end of his line for all he was worth, which naturally attracted the attention of all them city fishermen, not to mention setting that hook deeper into Arlo's poor thumb. Well, them genteel sportsmen crowded around, like they always do when someone catches a fish on opening day, and they started casting right over that way, hoping to get in on the fun.

"Sid hollered at them to quit, and to get out of his way, but that only got them more excited. There must have been a dozen of them, whipping the water to a froth, casting all sorts of spoons, spinners, and plugs, even snatch hooks in that direction, hoping to snag onto whatever Sid was fighting."

"Oh my lord!" exclaimed Mattie, "did they …"

"Ahuh," grinned Doc, "*six* of 'em did. At least, that's how many hooks I took out of various portions of Arlo's anatomy. And as he was at the time concentrating on getting *away* from all that excitement, you can imagine just which portions of said anatomy I had to concentrate on for a couple of hours last evening! That wet suit is going to need a lot more duct tape before he uses it again!

"In the fracas, a whole bunch of lines got tangled up, several of them got broke, including Sid's, and Old Gator got clean away! Sid was furious, but still doesn't know exactly what happened. He just figures them city folks got things so messed up that he lost his only chance at Old Gator for this season, not to mention his favorite fishing spoon!" He smiled again, "I've got it, of course, but I can't quite figure out how to get it back to him without a lot of explaining."

About that time the door bell chimed, and in slunk Merle and Arlo, all sheepish-looking. Arlo was limping like his hemorrhoids were bothering him pretty bad, and his thumb was all bandaged up.

Mattie had an awful time keeping her face straight as she said "Come on over and have a seat, guys, and I'll bring your coffee."

She and Doc both broke into gales of laughter when Arlo said, "No thanks, Mattie, I must have slept wrong, last night, and my back hurts – I think I'll just stand here by the counter, if you don't mind."

The End

Virgie

He wasn't a stranger. Most everyone in town knew him, but he was reclusive, so nobody thought too much about him, except to remark "There's old Seth! Didn't know he was still alive!"

His wife had passed on a couple of years ago, in her 90's, and Seth was pushing 100 by now; it's no wonder he didn't get around much.

So it was a surprise when he shuffled into Mattie's Place a few months ago, and went over to the booth where Doc and Big Jim were enjoying some of Mattie's blueberry muffins, and a pot of her best coffee.

"Well hello, old-timer," said Doc, "Come in and set a spell! What brings you out so far from home this morning?"

Old Seth nodded, stood there a minute, as if trying to decide which foot went first, and joined them. "Thanks, Doctor Howland, don't mind if I do." He looked at Jim, and continued, "But Jim's the one I came in to see. I asked at the newspaper office, and they told me you might be here. My great-granddaughter is home from college, so I asked her to drive me down to see if I could catch you."

Jim looked surprised, "Me, Seth? What can I do for you this morning?"

The old man smiled, and went on. "I never forgot your kindness to Virgie and me while she was in the nursing home, and even before that, and I got the idea you might like a keepsake from the both of us, just to remember her by." He accepted the cup of decaf that Mattie brought to him, and thanked her for the bran muffin as well. "Can't abide the seeds in the blueberry, you know."

Mattie greeted him with a hug, and a kiss on the cheek, and sat with them for a few minutes to chat. "You're more than welcome, Seth, it's on the house."

"You're all so good to me," said the old man, "since even before Virgie passed. She loved those Thanksgiving dinners that you used to send over with Lonnie." He paused a moment at the memory, "Then with Jim, here." She always wanted to get down here herself to help, but just couldn't do it. Strength was gone, with the arthritis and all. But that's not what I'm here for, as I told Jim and Doc."

He reached into a pocket and brought out a yellowed envelope, with faded handwriting and an old postmark on it. "Folks wondered how we met, and how we managed to stay together for over seventy years, and I thought you might like to know. You do some writing, don't you Jim? Maybe you could make a story out of this, just for Virgie. That would make me proud."

"Well, yes, I do write, a little," said Jim, "But I'm starting to run out of things to write about."

"Then here's an idea for you, if you've got time." The old man sat back in the booth, took another swig of the decaf, and began.

"Never did understand folks who don't believe in love at first sight, but we met back in school. I was 16, and Virgie was two years younger. We both were shy, but I guess she outgrew it first." He gave a wistful smile at that notion, and sat there for a minute, quietly recalling something on the far edge of memory. "Yes, I guess she did."

Seth looked at the envelope in his hand, and his finger traced the faint, graceful handwriting. Doc could make out Seth's name on it, but the rest was faded. The old man continued. "Everything is in here, Jim, all the bows and knots that she sent me while I was out west, even her picture. We saved them all these years, and I thought you might like the story behind them."

"Bows and knots, Seth?" Jim looked puzzled, but made no move to take the envelope. "I'm not sure I understand."

"Well, like I said, I was 16, and had quit school to work the farm. She lived in town, so the only times I got to see her was when we went in to the store, or once in a while at a social or a funeral, or at church. Her dad kind of discouraged us from getting too sociable. Wasn't mean about it, you understand, just not real encouraging. But he did hire me to do some work on his store, when things were slack on the farm."

"That's going back a long ways, Seth," said Doc, "I remember seeing that store all boarded up when I first moved here."

Seth smiled wistfully. "Yep, he didn't come through the Bad Times too well. Had a heart of gold, always tried to help, but there were just too many hurting people, and he finally went down with them.

"Anyway, Virgie worked summers, of course, in the store, and she was there when I went off to the Great War. She said she'd write once in a while, and I did get a letter or two, but mail was scarce over there, and we didn't hear from each other for a long while.

"Then when I got out of the Army, a fellow I had met in France talked me into going to Colorado with him. Said there was a fortune to be made out there. My folks were gone by this time, so I stopped back here to pick up some things, and make my goodbyes, and we headed west. I only saw Virgie once, and we didn't get to talk much, but it looked like she had been crying.

"It was nice out there, but the only job I could get was rough work in a mill, and it didn't leave me much time to make that fortune. Ted, that's my buddy from France, went to drinking, got sick, and died out there, but I stayed away from it. Then the letters started coming."

"Letters?" asked Jim. He pointed to the envelope in Seth's hand. "Letters like that one?"

"Yep," smiled the old man. "Letters. One a month, sometimes two. They weren't regular letters, like the ones that did manage to make it through to the front. Every one of them had a just a little slip of paper, with a little bow of colored ribbon pinned to it, and a bit of verse written on it.

"Sounds romantic," chimed in Mattie, "How sweet!"

"Yep, they certainly got my attention," smiled Seth. "The very first one said:

'If you are another girl's fellow,

Oh! send me back this bow of yellow.'

At first I didn't understand what in the world that was all about. But a few days later I got another one, and it hit me who they were from. "

The bell on the front door announced a new customer, and a radiant young woman entered, and looked around the diner. Her face lit up even more when she saw them, and she made her way over to the booth, smiling. "There you are, Grandpa Seth! I'm finished with my errands, so I stopped to see if you found your friend."

Seth beamed at the sight of her, and said "Hi sweetie! Sure did! Come over and have a seat! Jim, Doc, Mattie, this is my great granddaughter! She's the spitting image of her great grandma, and her name is Virgie too!"

Virgie said hello to the others, then turned to Seth and said "Are you about ready to come on home, grandpa? It's time for your meds, and for your nap. And I promised them that I'd have you back in time for Bingo. But I don't think they'll really mind, as long as you don't get too tired."

"Just like her great-grandma," complained Seth, with a big smile on his face, "Always keeping track of me. He peered into the envelope in his hand, and pulled out a yellowed photograph. See, just like her great-grandma."

"Oh my," whispered Mattie. "Spitting image is right! Look at that, Doc! If I didn't know better..."

"Absolutely!" said Jim, as the old man slowly got to his feet. "and I guess it must be you sent back the right color!"

"Well I sure did! I hand carried them all back, with a big bouquet of flowers, all colors but one! She carried a bouquet just like it at our wedding, and I gave her another just like it every anniversary since then. All colors but one! Got so Mr. Hanson, at the flower shop, would have it all ready for me, with all the right colors, every time I went in for it." The old man paused, and a shadow passed over his face, then he brightened again. "And he had one made up special for her funeral too, all the colors but yellow."

Old Seth went on to rejoin his Virgie a couple of weeks back, and they all went to the funeral. Doc and Mattie were there, along with half the town, it seemed. Jim gave the eulogy, and young Virgie spoke a few words too. Then she went up to the casket, kissed her great-grandpa on the cheek, tucked an envelope inside his jacket pocket, and put a bright bouquet in his hand ... every color but yellow.

The End

Virgie

'If you are another girl's fellow, Oh! send me back this bow of yellow.'

"If of me you love to think, send me back this knot of pink."

"If to me you would like to write, send me back this bow of white."

"If who sent these you wished you knew, send your Honey this knot of blue."

"If with me you would love to be seen, Return to me this bow of green."

"If to me you would like to be wed, In haste please send me this knot of red."

and last but not least, a paper with a lilac-colored bow on it:

"If with me you wish to elope, Send me back this heliotrope."

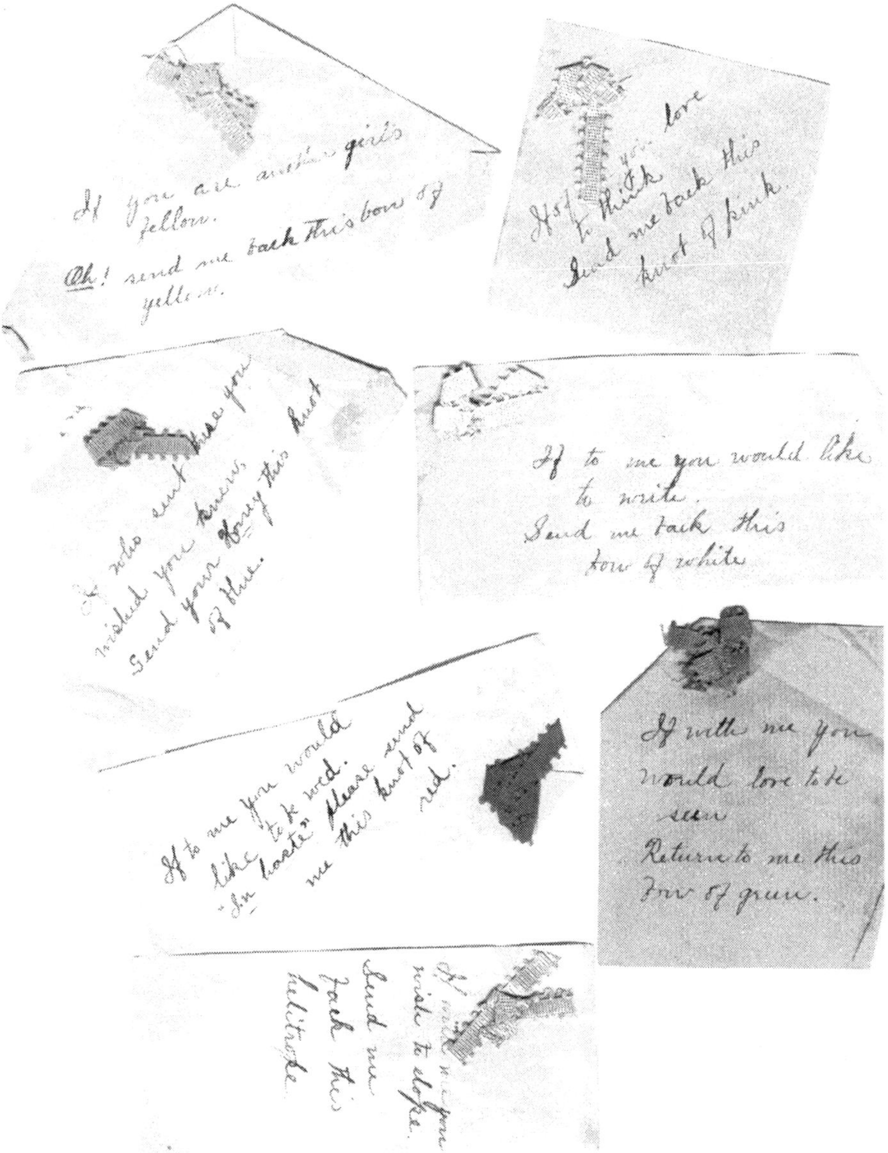
If you are another girl's
fellow.
Oh! send me back this bow of
yellow.
If to me you would like
to write.
Send me back this
bow of white
If to me you would
like to be wed.
"In haste" please send
me this knot of
red.
If with me you
would love to be
seen
Return to me this
bow of green.

Breinigsville, PA USA
15 March 2011
257667BV00001B/5/P

9 781935 268734